SMACK DAB
IN THE MIDDLE
OF MAYBE

JO WATSON HACKL

SMACK DAB IN THE MIDDLE OF MAYBE

RANDOM HOUSE 🏠 NEW YORK

Text copyright © 2018 by Jo Watson Hackl
Cover art and interior illustrations copyright © 2018 by Gilbert Ford

All rights reserved. Published in the United States by Random House Children's Books, a division of Penguin Random House LLC, New York.

Random House and the colophon
are registered trademarks of Penguin Random House LLC.

Grateful acknowledgment is made to Harvard University Press for permission to reprint lines from "A winged spark doth soar about" from *The Poems of Emily Dickinson: Reading Edition*, edited by Ralph W. Franklin, Cambridge, MA: The Belknap Press of Harvard University Press, copyright © 1998, 1999 by the President and Fellows of Harvard College. Copyright © 1951, 1955 by the President and Fellows of Harvard College. Copyright © renewed 1979, 1983 by the President and Fellows of Harvard College. Copyright © 1914, 1918, 1919, 1924, 1929, 1930, 1932, 1935, 1937, 1942 by Martha Dickinson Bianchi. Copyright © 1952, 1957, 1958, 1963, 1965 by Mary L. Hampson.

Photos on page 223 are from the author's personal collection, used by permission.

Visit us on the Web! rhcbooks.com

Educators and librarians, for a variety of teaching tools,
visit us at RHTeachersLibrarians.com

Library of Congress Cataloging-in-Publication Data
Names: Hackl, Jo., author.
Title: Smack dab in the middle of maybe / by Jo Hackl.
Description: First edition. | New York : Random House, [2018] | Summary: "When Cricket's aunt Belinda accidentally forgets her in the grocery store, Cricket decides to run away once and for all. But Cricket has to stay close by because even though her mama hasn't been in touch since she disappeared, she'll surely come back. And Cricket has to be there when she does. Because she needs answers"—Provided by publisher.
Identifiers: LCCN 2016018105 | ISBN 978-0-399-55738-5 (hardcover) | ISBN 978-0-399-55739-2 (hardcover library binding) | ISBN 978-0-399-55740-8 (ebook)
Subjects: | CYAC: Mothers and daughters—Fiction. | Runaways—Fiction.
Classification: LCC PZ7.1.H15 Sm 2018 | DDC [Fic]—dc23

Printed in the United States of America
10 9 8 7 6 5 4 3 2 1
First Edition

Random House Children's Books
supports the First Amendment and celebrates the right to read.

TO MY FAMILY,
WHOSE LOVE, FAITH, AND SUPPORT
MAKE EVERYTHING POSSIBLE

CHAPTER 1

FEBRUARY FIREHOUSE JUBILEE FISH FRY

Turns out, it's easier than you might think to sneak out of town smuggling a live cricket, three pocketfuls of jerky, and two bags of half-paid-for merchandise from Thelma's Cash 'n' Carry grocery store.

The hard part was getting up the guts to go.

It happened like this: There I was in Thelma's produce section, running my fingers up and down a bundle of collards. Collards never did make for good eating, but I was wondering if maybe they were some kind of sign that it was time for me to skedaddle. Collards always reminded me of Mama. She used to make me drawing paper out of collards, sumac seeds, dryer lint, and newspaper Daddy chopped up in his wood chipper. She plunked things in her paper the way other people stuck things in scrapbooks. Thread from the hem of her wedding dress, a four-leaf clover, Daddy's first gray hair. Mama's paper held so much life, it made my drawings pop right off the page.

That was the kind of mama and daddy I used to have.

I was ruffling up those collards, mourning my daddy and scheming on how to sneak away to win back Mama. Not that I had much time for scheming. Aunt Belinda, Little Quinn, Jackson, and Clay were the next aisle over. My cousins were working hard at plowing down every last tower of cans in that store. Aunt Belinda, she was working hard at keeping some distance between her cart and those crashes.

Me, I was supposed to be finding Aunt Belinda some hot sauce. She hadn't even started her potato salad *or* her red velvet cake, and already folks were busy unsnapping folding chairs, setting up for the fry. As in the February Firehouse Jubilee Fish Fry and Red Velvet Cake Cook-Off—the place where Aunt Belinda said she was *finally* going to land herself a new husband to take the place of Daddy's no-account brother. She already had her sights set on the new fireman, the one with the king-cab truck.

"Get your head out of the clouds, Cricket." Aunt Belinda knocked my hand off the collards. So much for signs. "Make yourself useful. I need that hot sauce. And call Aunt Fig and find out whether her cake recipe calls for buttermilk or sweet milk." She handed me her cell phone.

It came alive with the sound of "Love Me Like You Mean It."

Aunt Belinda grabbed back the phone. "WOKT Country is my favorite radio station," she chirped.

I rolled my eyes. Soon as Aunt Belinda got named a finalist for the Dollywood Trivia Trip of a Lifetime, she'd started answering her phone that way so she'd win if WOKT called.

Aunt Belinda ducked her chin and shuffled two steps back. "Can't talk now. This coming Wednesday. Got it."

She rambled through her purse, found the Post-it note with her to-do list, and scratched down two lines. Slapping the note on top of her purse, she looked at my bangs, not meeting my eyes. "Pecans are your favorite, right?" She threw a big bag in her cart, the expensive kind, not store brand.

My neck hairs went prickly.

With money too tight even for dollar-store art supplies, why was Aunt Belinda buying me things all of a sudden? Did she want me to do some more blind-date babysitting? I poked at the bag. "Who was that on the phone?"

Aunt Belinda just stared at the rutabagas, sucking her cheeks in like she was working on a mint. Finally, she yanked a tube of Wanda's Classy Lady Peach Passion lipstick out of her purse and jerked it across her lips. "Never you mind. Now get me that hot sauce. Pronto."

My cousins swarmed up and started prying the bottom okra can out of the pyramid display.

Aunt Belinda spun her cart around, and the sticky note flew off her purse.

"Hey, you dropped . . . ," I yelled after her, but she was already speeding toward the meat section.

I left the note right where it was. The sooner I found the hot sauce, the sooner we could *all* get out of the store.

But before I even got past the Duke's mayonnaise, I spotted her—a little brown cricket stuck in a spiderweb on the baseboard.

The poor thing was trapped even worse than me. She was trying to wiggle out and was tangling herself up worse. The spider skittered close.

I snatched that cricket loose.

Not fast enough.

I saved her from the spider, but Little Quinn swooped in like a duck on a June bug. "Look, Clay, Cricket's done found herself a cricket. Maybe they're related."

Twisting away, I studied the bug in my hand. It was probably her and her kin who'd been making music in our backyard all last summer.

After a minute, she figured out I wasn't going to hurt

her none. Her antennae relaxed, and she took a tiny step on legs as thin as embroidery thread. She looked like she was listening for something. Was she hoping for the sound of someone out there calling, calling, calling, and waiting for her to answer back?

Maybe I *did* have more in common with that bug than just a name.

The cricket turned her warm brown eyes on me and cocked her head. I swear she saw inside me and asked the same exact question I'd been asking myself for days: *Just how far will you go to get your mama back?*

Before I could even *think* about answering, Little Quinn pulled a firecracker out of his pocket and dug for the matches. "Hand her over." He sounded bored. It was just another blowing-things-up Saturday.

I kicked him in the shin, not hard enough to leave a bruise he could point at, just enough to get him out of the way. Pulling the cricket in tight, I shot for the door.

But Aunt Belinda wheeled up and pointed at me with a Trans Am–red fingernail. "Put that nasty thing down and find me that hot sauce." She plopped a loaf of white bread in her cart and cut her eyes toward the store clock, its hands almost at noon. "You know they're shutting up early for the fry."

"Just a minute. I need to . . ."

Aunt Belinda tilted her face toward the greasy ceiling

tiles. "Lord, please save me from selfish children." Then her voice turned into the one she used when she was trying to get her boys to bed. "Just help me out this one time, Cricket. For the fry. Will you do that much?"

"Yes, ma'am," I sighed, trying to get out of hearing, for the umpteenth time, all the things Aunt Belinda used to do to help out *her* family when *she* was twelve.

My cousins swaggered closer, blocking the way to the door. I had to get the cricket out if she was going to make it.

"Gotta go." I swerved toward the bathroom.

The back lights were already off, and I fumbled for the bathroom switch. One tiny window glowed on the rear wall, the glass painted in the same overcooked butter-bean color as the rest of the store. A slice of light showed through the bottom, though, where the window was pushed out. Just big enough for the cricket.

That was the good news. The bad news was, the window was too high to reach. A tall trash can stood next to the door. I waltzed it side to side over to the window, holding my breath against the smell of dirty diapers, Comet, and wet brown paper towels.

"Cricket, I hope you're grateful," I whispered.

She wasn't.

Soon as I opened my fingers to check on her, she sprang onto the lightbulb over the mirror.

I wriggled my way onto a sink, prayed the whole thing

wouldn't fall off the wall, and tried to coax her loose before she got burned.

Instead, she catapulted onto the top of a stall. Balancing on a lopsided toilet seat, I lunged after her. Aunt Belinda was going to kill me for taking so long.

By the time I finally caught her, we'd visited all four toilets once and some two times.

I was out of breath and really, really needed to wash my hands.

But I'll say one thing for that cricket—she had a mind of her own. "Names carry a power," Daddy always said. Right then and there, I picked out a good one for her— Charlene. Mama's middle name.

Hoisting myself onto the trash can rim, I pushed the window open wider and started to let Charlene out. But instead of clean air, I got slapped with the smell of fresh-poured asphalt from the side parking lot. Charlene would get stuck in the tar. I'd have to take her out the front. I eased the bathroom door open.

The store was dark, too dark.

It was too quiet.

It was too empty.

It took me about a minute to figure out that the only living creatures in the store were me and that cricket.

She stared at me with those question eyes of hers, waiting on me to make the next move.

CHAPTER 2

FRESH MEAT

A red neon sign over the meat counter crackled on and off. FRESH MEAT. FRESH MEAT.

Maybe Aunt Belinda's waiting in the car.

But the parking lot was empty, too.

I got a carsick feeling.

This was low-down, even for Aunt Belinda. How could she leave *me* before I had a chance to leave *her*?

What made me even madder was, I should have had the good sense to see the whole thing coming. I could just picture Aunt Belinda leading the bag boy out to her Mustang, my cousins wrestling all the while. I could see Aunt Belinda cranking up Lucinda Williams and flooring it for the dirt road off the highway. She probably wouldn't think one thought about me until it was time to unload the car and start me peeling potatoes. By then, she'd be eighteen miles away, with nothing but one long dust cloud between her and Thelma's.

Something crackled under my foot.

Aunt Belinda's grimy Post-it list.

Hot sauce, potatoes, milk, red food coloring
Make red velvet cake and potato salad
GAG—Wed. 3:30
Cricket pack

My carsick feeling shifted into fifth gear.

GAG. My nickname for Great-Aunt Genevieve. What had Aunt Belinda said on the phone? "This coming Wednesday." Those words rolled through my body, fast as a marble through one of those runs me and Mama used to build when I was little.

Every syllable struck me at some fresh, sharp angle.

Clang. GAG wasn't my great-aunt, no matter what she claimed. More like my second cousin twice removed. She hadn't bothered to show up for Daddy's funeral, but she'd sent word right quick she'd be happy to take in me and my Social Security check.

Clang. GAG lived in a trailer park ten miles outside of

town. In *Kentucky*. If Aunt Belinda sent me off to live with her, I'd never make it back in time for Mama.

Clang. I had to get away and hide out until Mama came back. But where?

Clang. Since Keisha moved to Mobile, there wasn't anybody I could stay with. Even if you're *not* in and out of homeschool all the time, best friends aren't exactly easy to come by. I couldn't hide out in town. Someone would recognize me and send me back to Aunt Belinda. And Aunt Belinda would send me to GAG.

Clang. Aunt Belinda had rented out our old house. There was nowhere to go.

The marble went into free fall, landing with a *thud* at the base of my spine.

My breath started to get away from me. I was about to miss my chance to see Mama. Then the idea came: Daddy's woods.

The woods smack dab in the middle of nowhere. Nobody around for miles.

The woods not far from where Mama would be. And those very woods might be holding the one thing I needed to get Mama to stay for good.

I looked down at that tuckered-out cricket.

Is she the sign I've been looking for?

I still hadn't answered her. *Just how far will you go to get your mama back?*

10

I couldn't stop Mama from leaving, and I couldn't stop Daddy from dying, but I could sure do something now. Grandma always said crickets bring luck. *Maybe my luck is changing.*

Daddy'd taught me about the woods. Okay, not everything. But Daddy and Granddaddy used to swear by the power of Woods Time. Would it work for me, too?

Daddy's book was already out there. It could help.

And everything important was right here on me. After Little Quinn blew my sketchbook to smithereens, I'd started toting around the things that mattered. Now I patted them one by one. I had the doogaloo in my jeans pocket. I was wearing Daddy's jacket, and his big pockets carried the rest—Daddy's pocketknife, the letter from the headstone company, my hat and gloves, and a little notebook full of Mama's paper. Plus, I had my money.

If I hurried, maybe I could beat the dark.

Then I started thinking about the cold waiting just outside the grocery-store glass.

I'd never been out in those woods without Mama or Daddy.

Aunt Belinda would be home in another twenty minutes. I could call her to come pick me up.

Charlene chirped three quick times, her notes high and fine and clear.

There she was, cupped in my hand in the middle of Thelma's, and she was still putting out music.

"Leave." I said it so loud, it bounced back at me off the concrete walls like somebody else was doing the talking.

Me and Charlene, we could do this together.

The sign over the meat counter slung washed-out shadows over the shelves. My steps echoed on the sticky floors. As creepy as the whole place was, though, part of me liked it. It was the first time since Daddy died that I didn't have to put on my "I'm okay/don't ask" face. It was the first time since Mama left that whispers weren't buzzing around me, the entire sixth grade wanting to know why Mama ran off. It was the first time in a month of Sundays without Aunt Belinda rushing me or my cousins pestering me.

I fluffed out two bags from behind the cash register.

The Little Debbie snack cakes called to me, but I was good. I only took two boxes. For the rest, I went with what Daddy would have picked—jerky, apples, peanut butter, an emergency candy bar, plastic cups, duct tape, matches, clothesline, a hand shovel, tissues, underwear, and socks. We didn't have a sleeping bag out there, so I grabbed two sweatshirts to keep warm. My big splurge was a pack of number two pencils and a sharpener. I'd go crazy in those woods if I couldn't draw.

The pencils almost made up for the *Who Farted?*

sweatshirts, which, I'm sad to say, were the only kind Thelma had.

I made Charlene a nest out of two duct-taped cups and a tissue, and punched in some breathing holes. Putting my cash by the checkout, I did the math. When I came up short by half, I started a column in the notebook: *Money I Owe: $36.47 to Thelma's Cash 'n' Carry.*

I leaned my weight into the back-door exit bar and stepped out into the clouded-over afternoon.

"Charlene," I said, "let's go get Mama back."

CHAPTER 3

THE OTHER SIDE

If you're going to take to the woods with nothing but a bug for company, do it on the day of the fry. I didn't draw one speck of attention on the way out of town. Pickups loaded with fish fryers, minivans loaded with families, they all blew right past me.

Besides that fry, I had three things going for me.

One, it was still hunting season. Folks were used to seeing people trotting on the side of the highway, looking between those straight rows of trees for something to shoot at. I hugged Daddy's jacket tight, tucked my hair in the collar, and picked up a broke-off branch. Every time I heard a car coming, I pulled my hunter's orange hat down a smidgen more, held that branch under my arm the way you'd hold a rifle, and turned my head toward the pines. People see what they want to see. I looked like a hunter, maybe just a smallish one.

Two, Daddy's camouflage jacket worked for me. The pockets handled most of the supplies and the cricket cups, too. The bags thumping against my leg handled the rest just fine.

Three, I never was one to stand out in a crowd. I used to be jealous of Keisha, the way every head turned toward her bright brown eyes. Now I was glad for the way I looked—eyes more gray than blue, freckles scattered like the pattern on Daddy's jacket, my hair always a summer away from being blond. It was like I was born ready to blend into the woods.

And I knew where I was going.

Or I thought I did.

I'd spent enough time there with Daddy. There were two ways to go. If I stuck to the main roads, it would be over fifteen miles. But if I turned off on the dirt road and cut through the woods, it would only be nine miles. Me and Daddy, we'd done a 10K walk the last time Mama was in the hospital. This wasn't *that* much farther.

Either way, I was heading south. It seemed to me somehow like it should be easy, like walking down the globe in science class.

Wrong.

It was mostly anthills and briars.

Those briars made me worry about search dogs. Was I a runaway now? True, Aunt Belinda had left *me,* but would that matter? Every couple of miles, I backtracked and went around in crooked figure eights. I saw on a science show once that a bloodhound can track your smell across just about anything. Your only hope is to make the handler think the dog lost your trail. That or let your trail go stale.

Aunt Belinda wouldn't want to admit I'd run off. It'd make her look bad in front of that fireman she liked. That'd buy me some time. But they'd sure enough notice me missing from school come Monday morning.

With every weed I brushed by, all I could think about was how long my scent would cling to those sticky stems.

I made some extra figure eights, just in case.

The whole walk, I tried to keep Mama in my head, to see this weedy patch the way she would.

Meandering with Mama while Daddy was offshore was like wearing a special pair of glasses, part binocular, part microscope. Mama never *walked* anywhere. She ambled. She skipped. She strolled.

"Walking is for other people," she always told me.

"What people?" I would ask.

"Those people. People who don't see things the way we do. We're *meanderers,* Cricket. We pay attention."

Mama would have noticed the way the clouds were starting to look like curled-up cats and the way the crows were flying from tree to tree in front of me. She would have noticed the sweet smell of tea olive trees and walked forever to pick a sprig for my room. She would have braved the thorny branches above my head to bring me back the last wild orange.

Now I shivered as the wind pecked at my cheeks, the turnoff to the old dirt road just ahead.

The rows stopped by the barbed wire fence. Behind us, row after row of same-size timber-company pine trees stretched as far as I could see. In front, the woods turned wild. Hardwoods, pines, briars, and bushes, they all crowded out the light.

Brushing up against a sumac bush, I broke off a handful of seeds, breathed in the smell of Mama's paper, and wedged my way through the barbed wire.

Overhead, birds started squawking. They didn't like me and Charlene invading their woods.

The only thing left of our path was the small gap in the briars. I followed it, tossing the seeds ahead of me, one by one.

I tried to keep what I could see of the sun on my right side. "The sun sets in the west," I whispered to Charlene. "This way, we know we're heading south." With each step, though, it seemed like that sun was slanting at us lower.

I hiked faster.

The path ended at the rickety, narrow footbridge.

The water was running high. Already it had rotted out two boards, and the rest were so loose, they might not be there tomorrow.

Still, it was the only way.

Tucking Charlene close, I crawled across the sagging wood.

My foot hit the bank, and Charlene let out a chirp. She knew it, too.

We were on the other side now.

CHAPTER 4

A HUNDRED AND FIFTY YEARS OF DARK

The woods smelled like a hundred and fifty years of dark. A goose-bumpy ghost-town kind of dark.

It didn't feel right to be here without Mama and Daddy.

The trees all looked the same—rough barked and winter bare. No sign of where our path used to be.

Nothing felt familiar, not even me.

Scanning the treetops, I tromped through the thick leaves, searching for the clear spot that marked the old logging road.

When I finally found the break in the trees, I was worn out and sweaty, with panic starting to buzz in my brain, loud as those bird squawks.

Then I saw the sign.

Back before the logging road got grown over, the state had put up a plaque. Now the sign was faded and off kilter, but I could still read the words.

ELECTRIC CITY, MISSISSIPPI

**Site of one of our nation's
premier electric lumber mills.
In 1920, the Electric Lumber Company
purchased cutting rights to hundreds of
thousands of acres of timber from nearby
landowners. The company built the mill
and a modern town with a central park,
a theater, a library, a general store,
a teaching hospital, and attractive homes.
The town even minted its own currency,
the doogaloo. When the timber
was harvested decades later,
the company removed the buildings.**

Mama and Daddy always called it a ghost town, and Daddy's family still squabbled over whether they'd done the right thing all those years back, teaming up with the neighbors to grant those cutting rights.

Everywhere I looked, something reminded me of

the way things used to be—the thick-poured sidewalks stretching out in neat squares for miles, the old home-sites taken over by scraggly pines, the honeysuckle vines hugging the concrete pillars that used to prop up the houses.

I tried to picture the way it was when Daddy lived here, the sidewalks bustling with people headed to work, to shop, to see a show, going home to street after street of crisp white houses and clean-kept yards.

How could they just take everything away?

A cracked cement front walk led to a set of columns just ahead—all that was left of Daddy's old home. Three wide steps ended in empty air. THE OVERLANDS was still etched on the top step. The steps Daddy, Uncle Quinn, Mawmaw, and Granddaddy posed on in all those photos from when Daddy was little.

I put a pebble on the top step, just like Daddy always did.

The whirling leaves made whisper sounds, pointing out things to notice.

That straight line of pillars from the movie theater, the sidewalk there edged in quartz rocks. Daddy'd told me how these rocks used to catch the moonlight. Past that, I saw the pillars that used to hold up the old library and the general store.

Me and Charlene followed the third sidewalk to the left for three-quarters of a mile. There, in the only ginkgo tree in the woods, I saw the one thing me and Daddy ever finished together.

"Look, Charlene," I said. "Our new home."

CHAPTER 5

NO MATTER WHAT

Our tree house stood seven feet off the ground, tucked so tight between the branches that you'd walk right past it if you didn't know what you were looking for.

I recollected the day last spring when Mama and Daddy put me to work hunting for just the right tree. "Make sure you stay on our family's land. And look for sturdy," Daddy said.

"But pretty." Mama slid her cool fingers across my cheek. "Always seek the beauty."

"And made of tough stuff like you?" I fake-punched Daddy.

"It doesn't have to be quite as handsome." He pointed

to a towering tree. "Bodock. Listen to the wood." He rapped the trunk with my knuckles. "What do you think it's saying?"

"That it's too bumpy. Let's pick something else."

We walked half the morning until I spotted that ginkgo tree. Its limbs spread out, inviting me to climb up on in. In the speckled sunlight, its fan-shaped leaves quivered in sixteen shades of green. "This is it," I said.

"Don't forget to build me a porch." Mama tucked a leaf behind my ear, put one behind hers, and headed off bird-watching.

"Not too many tree houses you can get to by sidewalk." Daddy picked up his hammer.

He used the right nails, four on each rung, for the ladder. Over the next few weekends, we measured off the walls, seven feet each, exactly. We waterproofed the roof. We added shutters to the window cutouts so we could take pictures out the windows whenever we wanted and could close the shutters at night to keep out the bugs. We shored up the beams with steel plates. "Can't be too careful," Daddy always said.

Fat lot of good it did him.

After Grandma died last summer, Mama went to pieces. Come winter, Mama up and ran off. It wasn't even twenty-two full days before the principal called me out of study hall. Later, after Aunt Belinda ran all those red lights on the way to the hospital, after they wouldn't even let me see my own daddy, after all of it, that doctor stood in scuffed-up Docksides dangling Daddy's chart, staring at the wall behind me and Aunt Belinda. "There wasn't anything we could do," he said. "It was like his own body turned against him. No way he could've seen it coming."

I let Aunt Belinda lead me out to the car, but I knew better. Thirty-eight years of clean living got undone in ten minutes by a blood clot that started out no bigger than a gnat too small to swat at.

With only me left, it was like there just wasn't enough weight to hold Daddy to this earth.

I shook that thought loose. Keeping Charlene close, I climbed the ladder.

The tree house smelled of cedar, clean and wild. Daddy'd put down old shag carpet to muffle our sound so we wouldn't scare off the wildlife before he had a chance to take their picture. Pressing my back into the floor, I breathed in deep. Mama had painted us a red, white, orange, and black calico heart on the wood above the door when she came for her third and last visit. I showed it to Charlene.

Now the color was fading.

My breath started to speed up.

So I pulled out the letter.

It was addressed to Mama and Daddy, and I knew it by heart. When that letter got written, nobody could have known there'd be another tombstone so soon—the ugly, cheap one Aunt Belinda bought for Daddy's grave over in his family's plot next to the Big Ridge Baptist Church.

December 1
Dear Mr. and Mrs. Overland:

We have scheduled the headstone for Mrs. Overland's mother to be delivered to the Pickens County Baptist Cemetery in Electric City at 9:00 a.m. sharp on the first of March. We will meet Mrs. Overland at that time to verify proper alignment.

We have never had the privilege of carving a headstone with movable interlocking pieces before. As you know, the intricate carvings Mrs. Overland designed have required considerably more time than originally anticipated. We apologize for the delay and hope that your family will continue to look to us for all your monument needs.

Sincerely,
Edward Josiah Honeycut

December first. That was the date on the letter. Mama left three weeks later. After Daddy died, I found that letter in his things before Aunt Belinda swept me up in a hug and told me I was family even if we weren't blood kin. She said to come live with her. But the next day she squeezed Mama's lucky aventurine ring on her finger, handed me Daddy's jacket, and threw the rest of his stuff in the dumpster behind the Burger Barn.

Now I ran my hands over the note Mama had written on the letter, the one and only message she'd left:

I'm off looking for my birds.

That's what she always said when she disappeared. But she'd circled *the first of March* and *Pickens County Baptist Cemetery*—the cemetery next to this ghost town. Next to that, she'd scrawled in big, black, mashed-down Sharpie letters—

Don't let them start without me.
I'll be there. No matter what.

No matter what. After Grandma died, Mama used to say a lot of things she might not remember later. She sprinkled them around like salt and pepper on a ripe tomato— things she wanted to do, things she meant to do. But she never, ever broke a "no matter what" promise.

Those last few days before she left, Mama must have told me a thousand times how she wanted just two things. One, she wanted to find the Bird Room she was always looking for. She wanted to prove it was real. Two, she wanted to be there when the gravestone got put up so she could align the carvings and make sure they were what she wanted—a message for our family.

Mama was coming to these woods on March 1. I had eleven days to prove the Bird Room was real, to prove to Mama I believed her. And if I could do that, then maybe, just maybe, I could get her to stay for good.

CHAPTER 6

THE BIRD ROOM

On the night of my seventh birthday, Mama fixed me a great big ice cream sundae for dinner with pecan pie for dessert. The sundae had my three favorite flavors, all homemade by Mama—peanut butter, banana marshmallow, and chocolate crunch. With Daddy offshore, it was just the two of us, and Mama didn't even eat. She just watched me, a grin playing on her face. Soon as I took the last bite, she looped her arm through mine and pulled me to our back porch. "This is your night, baby," Mama said. "The sky knows it, too." A full moon was just starting to show itself against the summer cotton-candy clouds, and

29

the air hummed with the sound of crickets, katydids, and tree frogs. It sounded to me like a parade.

"I want to tell you a story." Mama patted a spot next to her on the porch swing. "When I was little, I was smart, like you. My daddy used to bring me on his electrician jobs when I wasn't in school. I fetched him tools and kept him company on those long drives." She smoothed back the hair on my forehead. "My daddy was licensed in two states, and we traveled all over. We'd start out before daylight and cover one, two hundred miles in a day." Her mouth drew into a tight smile. "It was *my* seventh birthday, and by afternoon, we'd been all over. We came to a job far off. Daddy had a string of work in a fancy neighborhood. Our last job was at the biggest house of all. Daddy took a while, and I got to looking around." Mama took a long breath. "I looked through a keyhole and found a room where every-thing was alive."

"Alive?" I thought I'd heard her wrong.

"Yes, baby." Mama closed her eyes. "There were birds dancing on the walls, moving in the light. A skinny man with paint all over his clothes came out of that room and invited me in. Said his name was Bob."

Mama snuggled me closer. "That room had every kind of bird you can think of—cardinals, woodpeckers, humming-birds, doves, even crows. But the one I liked best was a watermelon-red bird with black wings. It fluttered its wings at me."

"What kind of bird was it?" I asked.

"Bob said it was a boy scarlet tanager and you have to be lucky to see one, even once. It mostly stays high in the treetops and flies through Mississippi only certain times of year, on its way to and from flying over a thousand miles to spend the winter in South America. In the fall, its red feathers start to turn green.

"Just imagine." She turned to look me straight in the eyes. "A bird that could change itself to fly someplace new."

Mama's eyes went to the tree line. "I knew it the instant I saw that bird—the world didn't have to be plain and boring. It could be bright and bold and exciting. I didn't have to settle for ordinary." Mama flicked a speck of dirt out from under her fingernail. "I wanted to be like that bird."

I grabbed her hand and held it tight. I wanted my mama to stay my mama. But for her, I tried to picture that bird changing colors and looking at the world from up high. "What else was in that room?"

Mama looked back at me. I could tell her mind was still in that room. "Everything. Flowers and trees and vines and squirrels and birds and fish. I told Bob it was my birthday and seeing that room was the best birthday present I ever got. That made him smile. He said I'd shown up at exactly the right time, and he made me promise to come back and see the room when he was done. He asked me if I liked puzzles, and I said yes. He told me that since it was my birthday, he was going to give me a present—he'd tell me a secret he hadn't shared with a single soul. He lowered his voice and said that after he finished the room, he was going to leave a clue trail. If I solved it, I'd find a buried surprise. Then he handed me this."

Mama pulled something out of her pocket and pressed it in my hand. "He said it was the first clue."

CHAPTER 7

ELECTRIC DOOGALOO

Mama had handed me a tiny, round painting, colored on both sides. It was just big enough to fit between the circle of my thumb and first finger. "Thanks, Mama." It felt cold in my hand and heavy for its size and was covered in green, black, and red paint, the colors blending into one another.

At first, it just looked blurry. But when I squinted at it, the faintest outline of a red bird with black wings appeared. It looked ready to fly off.

"A tanager," I said. "One of your dancing birds."

Mama grinned. "I knew you'd see it, baby."

"So, did you go back to visit the room? Did you solve the clue trail?"

Mama took my hand again, her grip tight. "No. When I told Mama and Daddy about it, they didn't believe me. You know how Grandma is—always telling me to get my head out of the clouds, to be more practical. She and Daddy said paintings don't come to life. Instead of a painting, all they saw was one big blur. They said it was just junk. Mama and Daddy started saying I was getting too excited over nothing. Later, they tried to put me on medicine for it. But my Bird Room is real, Cricket. It was alive. And one day I'll prove it. I won't stop looking till I find it."

Mama stroked her thumb across my first finger like she wanted to make sure I was still there. "But for now, this is a little piece of magic—just like you. I want you to have it. I've been waiting seven years to give it to you. You have the eye, baby. You can see it."

Every night since then, I slept with that painted tanager under my pillow. Even after I had to go live with Aunt Belinda.

Which was a mistake.

My very first Saturday there, I woke up to the sound of a firecracker exploding and all three cousins laughing their heads off and running. What was left of my painting was in the middle of my bedroom floor with blown-off paint chips all around it.

34

But maybe my cousins did me a favor.

Because when I went to pick it up, I saw what was under all those layers of paint—a metal coin. I flaked off the rest of the paint. The coin was shiny as a nickel, but like nothing I'd ever seen before. One side was almost all taken up with an outline of a lightbulb with little rays coming out from it, all in raised-up metal. Below the lightbulb, *Good for $1.00 in merchandise.* The other side read, *Not transferable. Electric Lumber Company, Electric City, Mississippi.*

I was holding a doogaloo, the coin they'd taught us about in school.

Those coins came from only one place.

Mama was wrong—that Bird Room wasn't in a house far away.

Something right here in this ghost town was tied to Mama's Bird Room.

CHAPTER 8

WOODS TIME

It's not every day you get to set up a clue-finding base camp and make it any which way you want.

I divided the tree-house ledges into our food shelf, our supply shelf, and our clue shelf. Mama would be here in eleven days to see that headstone. With the food from Thelma's and just a little bit of living off the land, I'd have enough to keep me going for clue finding.

I propped the doogaloo on my clue shelf. Me and Charlene, we'd fill in more clues later.

"We can do this," I told Charlene. Daddy always said these woods were his own private museum and general store. Something new to look at every day, and everything he needed. I'd make these woods my museum and store, too.

Okay, so I didn't exactly know how we were supposed to solve an over thirty-year-old clue trail. But Mama said the doogaloo was the first clue. And we were in the town where it came from. The Bird Room and the rest of the clues had to be close by.

I got busy. The food shelf was easy. The supplies took longer. Daddy's book was where he always left it, sealed in a plastic bag in the army surplus box in the corner. The book still smelled like Daddy—all Dial soap and sawdust—with a bit of the smoke smell from our hot-dog campfires. The bag his book had come out of could be a supply, so I put that on the shelf. The box held other things I might need—the skillet, pot, plates, silverware, cups, and a little roll of wire. I put them all on my supply shelf next to my matches, clothesline, and hand shovel.

I brought in some dirt and crunched-up leaves from outside and laid them in the box. "Your cozy house." I slid Charlene in.

We'd need blankets. I sawed off some waist-high pine branches with Daddy's pocketknife, the way Daddy showed me that time we forgot our sleeping bags. Laying the branches out straight, I ran a row of duct tape across them, turned them over, and did the same thing on the other side.

Using the last of the tape, I made a blanket lid for the top of Charlene's box.

To keep us extra warm, I hauled in some pine limbs and piled them against the walls. Pine needles should help hold in the heat, right? I added some berry sprigs I found for decoration. That part came from Mama. "Seek the beauty."

Next was water. Me and Daddy always toted that in with us, but a branch of the creek wasn't far, and I scooped up a panful of water. I'd need to boil it before I could drink it, so I grabbed the matches.

Beside the tree house, cement steps took me to a walk-in basement missing its house. Daddy'd told me the story about the mill superintendent's wife. Deathly afraid of tornadoes, she made them build her a full basement, complete with fireplace. The mill couldn't load up a basement, so they only took the top half of the house, floor and all. We'd added a grate Mama had welded to the fireplace for our campfires, and it still looked sturdy.

The woods gave me branches to break up to build a fire. In a way, it was like being back at Thelma's, picking things off the shelves. To tell you the truth, it was kind of fun.

Me and Daddy always started our fires with candle wax, dryer lint, and sometimes lip balm. "General store," I said, and scooped up two armfuls of twigs and dead leaves for kindling.

When the match caught, the flame threw off shimmering shadows. I couldn't believe it—I'd started a fire all by myself. For that one second, it felt like Mama and Daddy were right there next to me, cheering me on. I pushed three rocks into the fire. Daddy used to do that in our old fireplace to make foot warmers whenever we lost power.

The bird squawks had ended. An owl called. It didn't seem to mind me and Charlene being out here in the woods. A kink unhooked itself from my shoulders.

I'd beaten the dark.

Me and Charlene had a picnic on the tiny tree-house porch, the way me and Daddy used to do. It was cold, but we had us a proper meal, with apple, jerky, and a spoonful of peanut butter for me, and a sliver of apple for Charlene. If I stuck to two pieces of jerky a day, I could make it last till Mama.

For dessert, I savored every last crumb of one of the Little Debbies, no cousins around to take it. I eyed the candy bar, with its peanuts and caramel and chocolate deliciousness. Nope. I'd save that for later.

Squirrels chattered in a nest in the branches above us. So me and Charlene would have friendly neighbors.

"Tomorrow, we'll find more food," I told Charlene. "And we'll start looking for clues."

I pulled out Daddy's book to read up on things I

could eat. But something else caught my attention—notes in Daddy's handwriting next to certain sections.

WHEN CRICKET'S 12.

Sure enough, we'd already covered how to build a fire.

WHEN CRICKET'S 10.

Check. The different types of trees. Then I came to the part about living off the land.

WHEN CRICKET'S 13—WOODS TIME TOGETHER.

Those words hit me hard. Woods Time was here whether I was ready for it or not.

Just then, the first star appeared in the sky.

I leaned out to make a wish.

My wish was just one word—*Mama.*

I closed my eyes to make the wish extra strong. Soon as I did, though, I smelled something—hickory smoke. And it was closer than any fire should have been.

CHAPTER 9

THICK DARK

Nobody lived to the east, where the smoke came from. A second-cousin branch of Daddy's family used to own that part of the woods before they had a falling-out. Years of squabbling made sure that land stayed just as bare as it was the day the lumber company left.

Who is out there?

Campers? Hunters? Me and Daddy had run across hikers and hunters and their campfires out here from time to time. Was it somebody who might see my fire and turn me in for running away?

I climbed down, sprinted to the fireplace, scattered the coals, and ran back to the tree house.

Smoke from my fire squiggled into a question mark and faded.

Which left me and Charlene alone in the dark with the owl and the wind and who knew what else?

I couldn't see Charlene, but I heard her. She was hunkering down, drawing the dirt and leaves around her, bit by creaky bit.

Lying down on those sweatshirts, I drew the dark around me, too. I tried to think of Mama's songs, the way she'd sing "Amazing Grace" and sometimes Johnny Cash's "Ring of Fire." I tried to picture every little tug at the corner of her mouth the last time she sang to me, some clue that she was thinking about running off. Things I'd have noticed if I'd been paying attention good.

Charlene woke me up. *Yant, yant, YANT, yant. Yant, yant, YANT, yant.*

The sky was thick dark. Coyotes howled far off. From below us came sounds I couldn't put a name to. Sounds I might not ever *want* to put a name to. I was hoping it was just deer.

With Charlene next to me, though, I wasn't as scared as you'd think.

Charlene was missing somebody, too.

Hearing Charlene was like having somebody say, right out loud, something so deep inside me I hadn't found the words to put to it yet.

A single cricket answered back from deep in the woods, probably protected in an old homeplace. *Yant, yant, YANT, yant. Yant, yant, YANT, yant.* Charlene kept up her rhythm, but she didn't try to hop out of her box. Maybe it was enough just to know that somebody else was out there. *Yant, yant, YANT, yant.* I pretended it was calling for the both of us.

I heard the morning before I saw the light. Birds singing. Crows cawing to each other. Squirrels scampering on our roof.

The birds weren't squawking at us anymore. But everything felt off balance. My arm was asleep. My shirt stuck to my skin. My empty stomach churned. Aunt Belinda's house, even with my cousins and their Cheez Doodle fingers, sounded pretty good to me. If I were back there, Aunt Belinda would be standing at the stove in her electric curlers, frying up a mess of eggs and pouring us both coffee, making mine half cream.

The tiptoe morning light started sifting through the tree limbs.

No sign of smoke.

Charlene chirped, reminding me we needed to get started. But we'd need to be careful.

Ten days to find proof of the room Mama hadn't been able to find after a whole lifetime of searching.

But Mama hadn't known about the doogaloo. She'd probably been looking in the wrong places.

Still, how do you find a Bird Room in a town that's missing its houses? What if the Bird Room house got hauled off?

"We don't have to find the room," I told Charlene. "We just need to find something that *proves* the Bird Room used to be here."

I ate two pieces of jerky and set out for the sidewalks. Anything could be a clue. At each old homesite, I studied the columns, looking for a sign of . . . I didn't know exactly what. But something tied to Mama's room.

Block by block, I prowled. Nothing unusual. Just tipped-over pillars and overgrown yards.

My eye caught on a porch step. THE JOHNSON FAMILY. Four seashells.

Why hadn't I noticed that before?

I backtracked and started the search over, this time looking at the columns and steps, checking through the weeds for any more basements.

Lots of names. A few handprints, some pressed leaves,

44

and one dogwood flower were in the chipping concrete steps. Nothing that looked like it might be a clue.

By this time, my stomach was growling something awful.

I trudged back to the tree house and eyed the candy bar. "Just for an emergency," I told Charlene. I chomped into an apple instead.

I hadn't found a single clue all morning. If I was going to solve a whole clue trail, I needed to try something else. Then I remembered how Grandma loved to read mysteries. She always solved the clues before the end.

I'd go ask Grandma for help.

CHAPTER 10

HOPE IS THE THING WITH FEATHERS

All I could think about, as I dodged the cracks in the sidewalks on the way to the cemetery, was when I'd been there with Mama last summer. Mama didn't keep many regular habits, but visiting Grandma's grave was one thing she stuck to.

And that July day, Mama took me with her. She told me to wait in the car, but I wanted to be where Mama was. When I snuck out to find her, Mama was swaying over Grandma's grave. A propped-up plywood board stood where the headstone should have been.

Mama ran her fingers along the plywood. "I promised

you. I know I promised you." Her voice cracked, and she drew back like she'd just touched fire.

I couldn't watch. I slunk back to the car.

When Mama yanked the car door open, her face was hard. All the way home, she hung her hand out the window and parted the breeze back and forth, back and forth.

I just sat there watching Mama, hoping she wouldn't break her promise to Grandma. It never even occurred to me what other promises Mama might break.

Now I came up on the cemetery from the back way, those promises marching through my head. Grandma had said she'd made Mama promise her two things. One, that she'd stay on her medicine, keep her mood swings under control. Two, that she'd buy Grandma a proper headstone.

Promise number one didn't make it a full day after Grandma's funeral. Without Grandma there to count out the pills, Mama decided she didn't need them. Soon as Daddy pulled out of the driveway for the four-hour drive back to work offshore, Mama flushed her medicine. I found what was left of the capsules floating sideways in the toilet like little lost ships. Mama spent the whole next month propped up in bed with a pillow under her knees, the air conditioner turned up too high. She didn't say one word when I tiptoed in every evening to kiss her good night.

Mama worked harder at her second promise. After she finally got out of bed, just about all she did for weeks was make drawing after drawing of what she remembered about the Bird Room and drawing after drawing of Grandma's headstone.

I guess Mama figured a proper tombstone would make up for everything else.

Mama would keep her promise on March 1. Grandma would make her do it.

Now I pushed through the privet, climbed over the lean-to fence, and circled around to the front of the cemetery.

I could still read the sign, just the way I did last summer—HISTORIC PICKENS COUNTY BAPTIST CEMETERY. The sign gave directions to the new home of the Deerfield Baptist Church.

Standing there in the cold, I couldn't even remember the way it felt that day last summer—to have a mama and a daddy around without even thinking about it.

It was a wonder that time marched on like normal for anybody or anything else. It seemed to me that church sign should have been gone, faded back into the woods, eaten clear through by termites and rot.

Instead, the sign and the graveyard looked . . .

Tidy. That was it. No tumbled-down pillars. No weeds. Neat tea olive trees hugged the corners of the graveyard.

Our family's plot lay in the right corner. Two pieces of laminated paper taped to a plywood board laid out Grandma's life. *Beulah McLaurin Upchurch. Beloved wife. Hardworking mother. Faithful recording secretary for the Deerfield Homemakers Club.*

A Bible verse was printed in smaller letters: *May the Lord watch between you and me when we are absent one from the other. Genesis 31:49.* Grandma's favorite verse. The last words she ever said to Mama as Grandma typed them out on the paper for that temporary sign.

Soon as Grandma told Mama that the cancer had come back, that there wasn't any hope, Mama and Daddy stopped spending ten-dollar bills. Mama put every ten-dollar bill they came across in a Mason jar on the kitchen counter. She liked to have her money where she could see it. She got me to count out the bills every Friday morning at the kitchen table. She sat across from me, a copy of Leonardo da Vinci's *Codex on the Flight of Birds* propped open beside her, doing drawing after drawing of birds and headstone designs. Later, after she welded little models of the headstone parts, she sat there and tested them to make sure they lined up just right to catch the morning light.

At first, Grandma said Mama's way of saving was the most ridiculous thing she'd ever heard. But right after Mama passed the three-hundred-dollar mark, Grandma decided to join in. Grandma used twenty-dollar bills, not ten-dollar bills. She said she had some catching up to do, but me and Mama both knew better.

I know it sounds crazy for Grandma to compete with her own daughter to save up for her headstone, but Grandma's two favorite things outside of Bible verses, church meetings, and mysteries were planning ahead and being tight with money. I think she was happy to see Mama doing a little bit of both. Me, I was just happy to see them pulling together for once.

Grandma would make things right. She could fix everything from toilets to tractors. She was the one who always held Mama together. She'd bring my mama back here and make her stay for good.

I pictured Mama standing on this very spot, her face breaking out in that birthday smile of hers, soon as she caught sight of me.

"Look, Grandma." I held out the doogaloo. "I know you always thought Mama made up the Bird Room, but Mama's not going to stop leaving until she proves it's real." I told Grandma about figuring out about the doogaloo, about Charlene, about getting left in Thelma's, and about the tree house. "But I don't know where to look. If I ever needed your help, Grandma, I need it now."

Right that instant, a big red cardinal landed on the fence post and let out with his *chit-chit* call. *"Hope is the thing with feathers."* Mama said that every time she saw a cardinal. "Emily Dickinson wrote that in a poem." She said that every time, too. Mama called cardinals good-luck birds because they're easy to find when you need a smidgen of beauty. They're kin to tanagers but don't fly off to South America for the winter.

I didn't know if cardinals really *were* good-luck birds, but, seeing the red and the bright just then, it was about as close to good luck as I was likely to get out in these woods. I took it as a sign from Grandma. She'd help.

I started back to looking. I hadn't found anything on the sidewalks. Maybe there was something in this graveyard. It was the oldest thing in these woods.

I crouched at every grave.

Roger Earle Jason. A chain with three links. *Beloved husband and father.*

Tucker Grady Parker. A dove. *Departed this earth too young.*

One concrete tombstone had a rusted bed frame around it. No name, just initials—S.W. A dark, flat rock with a barely there carving was propped against it. The rock didn't match the color of the tombstone. I picked it up.

Wait. If I squinted real hard, the carving almost looked like a feather.

Could it be part of the clue trail Mr. Bob had told Mama about?

 CHAPTER 11

CLUE-SPROUTS

Whatever it was, it looked worn, like it had been sitting here all these years, just waiting for me to find it.

I looked closer. Was that writing below the feathery lines?

I turned it every which-a-way, but I couldn't read it. It looked to be in another language or some kind of code.

All of a sudden, it struck me—in a funny way, it made sense. If this rock really *was* part of Mama's clue trail, it wouldn't be easy to read. I'd have to solve it.

It brought to mind Daddy's words: "General store and museum." Maybe the rock was like something you'd find in a museum, something it took time to decipher. I'd work on it back at base camp with Charlene.

I felt sort of fizzy. I'd found a real clue! "Thanks, Grandma."

My stomach picked right that minute to start putting out a racket. I needed to go back and eat some more jerky.

But what if I ran out of food before Mama came back?

I thought about the church potluck lunch we always had after the service. I could be there now, eating three kinds of fried chicken, deviled eggs, potato salad, and all the carrot cake I could carry.

I couldn't give up now. I had to find food to keep me going for more clue finding.

I looked for the two plants I could remember that Daddy's book said I could eat—chickweed and greenbrier vines. I didn't find neither one.

Then I saw the tracks—three triangle lines with dots in the middle, the dirt scuffed up around them.

Turkey. Daddy'd taught me about their tracks.

Those turkeys must have been scratching for food. There had to be something to eat close by. But all I saw was a bunch of wild bamboo.

Something clicked inside my brain.

Bamboo! Mama loved to eat at Weidmann's Restaurant in Meridian. Their spring rolls had bamboo shoots inside them, and we always ate the rolls with peanut butter dipping sauce.

Maybe I could eat this.

But what we ate in the restaurant didn't look anything like what I saw growing in front of me.

I thought about it. Didn't "shoots" mean new sprouts? That had to mean they were just coming out of the ground, right?

When I studied the dirt, I saw little cones sticking up. The shoots! I sliced off the low cones with Daddy's pocketknife and peeled back the papery purple leaves. The white inside looked close to what I'd had in that restaurant. I touched it to my tongue.

It tasted raw, sort of like straw. If I cooked and sliced it like in the restaurant, it'd probably taste better.

I sliced off more shoots, enough to fill two pockets.

Another clump of bamboo bunched up around a pin oak tree. I pushed it aside, looking for sprouts.

An unblinking wood eye stared straight back at me.

CHAPTER 12

A WING AND A PRAYER

The eye peered out from a thick tangle of vines.

Underneath, a feather pattern was etched in the tree bark. A feather, like on my rock!

I started clawing back vines.

A beak. A bird.

A great big wide tanager eye looked me full in the face. I could tell it was a tanager by the short, rounded bill and by the way the carvings turned tighter and darker on the wings and tail.

Mama's tanager!

It was real and it was right here with me in these woods. Another clue!

The tanager curved around half the tree, its wings spread out like it was about to fly off. The carved part was dried out and crusted, and the tree bark had grown back over the edges. This carving was old, probably as old as the room my mama had seen.

A thousand thoughts swooped at me, but this was the biggest one—Mama hadn't been imagining things. I was following a clue trail: the feather in the rock and now two tanagers—on the doogaloo and this tree. There had to be another tanager—on the walls of Mama's Bird Room.

I couldn't wait to see Mama's face when I showed this to her.

I pulled more vines and my breath caught. A carved star was just under the tanager's beak, with slanty letters below:

WORTHY #3

I thought back to Mama's story of the Bird Room. I couldn't remember anything about a Worthy #3.

Ripples raced through my head. Had Mama seen this carving?

No, or she'd have told me.

Had Daddy?

No, or he would have brought me and Mama to see it.

It was up to me to figure out how this tree was linked to the Bird Room.

And if there was a Worthy #3, there had to be a Worthy #1 and a Worthy #2.

Right?

CHAPTER 13

CRITTERS

I pranced down the sidewalks, patting my bulging pockets and rubbing my fingers across that rock.

I figured I deserved a celebration lunch. I couldn't wait to dig into the jerky, an apple, and some bamboo shoots dipped in peanut butter. Maybe just one little nibble of chocolate off the end of my candy bar.

Rustling came from the direction of the tree house. Squirrels. They were probably thinking about lunch, too. We could have one big picnic in our tree.

But the closer I got to the tree house, the louder the ruckus.

Snarls and banging. Thumps from something bigger than any squirrel.

Saliva growls filled the air.

My throat went tight.

Charlene was in the tree house all by herself.

I ran.

A great big raccoon scurried down our ladder, dragging a strand of jerky. Two other raccoons chattered behind, holding something in their mouths.

They had my food!

I tore after them, into bushes, through straw grass, pines, and briars.

The raccoons disappeared behind thick blackberry brambles. No sign of them.

I didn't want to look. I didn't want to see.

But I'd left Charlene all alone.

I climbed the ladder and pulled back the lid to her box.

Charlene was jumping up against the sides like she'd been trying to fight the raccoons off.

I picked her up and stroked her across the back. "It's okay. It's okay."

Her antennae smoothed down. My heartbeat started to slow.

Then I saw.

Mama's paper was knocked off the shelf, next to the pencil and sharpener. They were all scratched up. My pine-branch blanket looked like it'd been pawed through. Wet, raggedy wrappers littered the floor. The apples were gone. And the jerky. And the Little Debbies.

My matches were chewed into tiny, useless bits.

My eyes darted around. The only food left was the peanut butter, the jar battered from where the raccoons had tried to break into it.

My candy bar—there wasn't even one lick of chocolate left on the bit-up wrapper.

My emergency candy bar was gone.

Still, my eyes kept searching. At first my brain didn't register what else I was looking for.

Then I knew.

Daddy's book!

Maybe the raccoons had just knocked it out of the tree house. I slid Charlene back into her box, climbed down the ladder, and combed through the bushes.

A flash of color shined through the brittle stems. *It will all be okay. I have the book.*

I snatched it up.

The cover was still attached. And so was the spine. And a few pages at the back about fish traps and cleaning fish. But the heart of it, the part with Daddy's notes, the part telling what plants could feed you, what plants could kill you, it was all gone—chewed up and shredded, just like everything else I thought we could live on.

60

CHAPTER 14

GLORIOUS LINT

"Sometimes you have to make do with what you have," Daddy said last summer. "Did you know you can make fire out of water? Let's try that. It'll get our mind off things." Daddy's book was lying beside him in our backyard. He took a plastic bag of water, pressed out the air, angled the bag into a cone, and tilted it in the sun. I squatted next to him, trying to pay attention. It had been a week since Grandma died, and Mama still hadn't said one word in my direction.

The bag flashed in the sun over a tinder pile Daddy had made from dryer lint, old Christmas candles, and dry grass.

"You try." Daddy turned my hand. The sunlight focused thick and thin, thick and thin.

A sharp beam shot out of the side of the bag and landed on the tinder.

Smoke curled up.

Daddy breathed steady breaths until a bright flame appeared. He fed it twigs, then branches.

"Did I ever tell you how I got your mama to marry me?"

I shook my head. I'd heard the story before, but I loved hearing him tell it.

Daddy leaned back. "First time I ever saw your mother, she was holding a blowtorch, about to weld a car axle, four pieces of angle iron, and eighteen yard-sale spoons into a sunflower sculpture." Daddy warmed his hands near the fire. "She had an eye like nobody else I'd ever met. I signed up for a photography class taught by a drunk man out of the back of his pickup truck just so I could be around her. I took up bird-watching. I took up *poetry*." He shot me a look. "Your mama ran circles around me. She had a documented sighting of a red-cockaded woodpecker. She read Faulkner. And while I was trying to get the hang of shutter speeds, your mama was off taking close-ups of butterfly wings. You know"—he stretched out a leg—"I asked your mama six times to marry me before she finally said yes. I tried everything. I got down on one knee. I promised I'd build this house, just where she wanted." He pointed at the logs stretching across our back porch. "I even bought this hat." He tilted the brim of his Stetson. "You know how your mama has a weakness for a man wearing the right kind of hat. Still, she put me off, said she wasn't ready. Said *I* wasn't ready."

"So, what'd you do?"

He cut his eyes toward the thick stand of trees where the land sloped down. "I did what my daddy did before me. Woods Time."

"But Grandpa was just trying to prove to himself he had what it took to support a wife before he went off and joined the army." I'd heard that story, too. "You already had a good job."

Daddy drew his mouth tight. "True," he said. "But I think I needed to learn what the woods had to teach me. When you're around other people, it's easy to get caught up in everything and everybody around you. Out in the woods, it's just you. And if you're going to last any time out in the woods, you'd better get comfortable with who-ever it is you are."

His eyes shifted toward the window. "I think your mama could tell there was something different about me when I got back. Woods Time made me think about what's important. I realized how your mama always notices things other people pass over, like those butterfly wings. She pays attention. And I figured if I was going to be able to be a good husband, I'd better start paying attention, too. Woods Time made me figure out how important the Bird Room was to your mama. Right off, I told her I believed her. She didn't even wait for me to ask her to marry me again." He leaned close. "She asked *me*."

"Can you show me how to do a Woods Time sometime?"

He laid his big, warm hand on my shoulder and scribbled something in his book. "Sure thing, honey. Whenever you're ready."

Now I clutched the plastic bag that had held Daddy's book and squatted over the clearest patch of sunlight I could find near the basement fireplace. I prayed that bag would help me make a fire to keep me and Charlene warm and boil our water. Tilting the bag over a little bed of dried-up grass, leaves, and twigs, I studied the clouds above me and waited for the warm beam of light.

No beam.

I couldn't do this without Daddy.

Everything inside me sagged. I was already tired from tromping through the woods all afternoon looking for more bamboo shoots so I could make the peanut butter last longer. My stomach rumbled. I recollected the way that Little Debbie cake tingled on my tongue the night before, and that made it all the worse.

From the direction of the tree house, though, I heard Charlene's chirping.

She was out here with me.

I tried to go over every little step in my head.

"I've got the bag." I'd skimmed clear water from the top of the creek for it.

"But no tinder like the lint and candle wax Daddy used." Even Aunt Belinda's greasy lip balm would have come in handy now. "What else?"

I sprinkled dried leaves and grass on the twigs. Holding my breath, I turned the bag. A thin slice of sunlight flashed, then disappeared.

I tried again.

Another beam, thicker this time.

I focused it. Smoke wavered out of the tinder pile.

A flame flickered, smaller than a wish.

I gave it a jerky breath.

The smoke trailed out, leaving behind nothing but black leaf-skeleton bits.

The sun was getting lower. I scooched over to chase the sunlight.

Why hadn't I put even one match in my pocket to keep it safe?

I got some fresh water, new dried-out leaves and grass and twigs, and tried again.

Maybe it was too cold out.

I reshifted the plastic and waited for the ray. This time, I focused it on the dried grass.

After forever, it started smoking.

The fire fizzled out.

I scrambled around for a backup plan. Something else I could try.

From the tree stand, Charlene chirped. *Don't give up.* We'd come this far. We'd found the feather rock. We'd found the tanager tree.

I jammed my hands into my jeans pockets to warm them up before I tried again.

My right finger hit something—the fluff from Aunt Belinda's dryer.

Lint! Thick, glorious dryer lint!

I scraped every bit out of all five pockets of my jeans and the six pockets of Daddy's jacket. Stretching that lint, I kneaded it, whispered to it, and spread it out flat.

I wrapped the lint over the driest grass and willow twigs and leaves I could find, laid them on a piece of flat pine-tree bark, and tried to catch the light.

When the smoke finally came, I gave it a steady breath.

A flame spread.

I cradled the fire, did a slow, careful shuffle to the fire-place, and fed it more twigs and branches.

Slowly, it grew until it could stand on its own.

The heat warmed my hands and flushed my face. I

propped three more branches on top, crouched in close, and brought Charlene over to see it all.

Me and Charlene, we sat and watched our fire. It swayed in orange, red, yellow, and blue flames, like some kind of rainbow you'd dream up in your head.

Fire I'd started.

Fire I'd grown with my own two hands.

CHAPTER 15

CLEAR AS A
MUD PUDDLE

Sitting up in the tree house with Charlene, our stomachs full of peanut butter and bamboo shoots, it hit me—that gang of raccoons hadn't beaten me. The woods had thrown a test at me, and I'd passed. I was winning at Woods Time.

I could do this! I picked up the rock and turned it every which-a-way. I would figure it out. But no matter how long I stared, no matter how many different ways I turned the rock, I couldn't make out any words. The carving was too faint.

Grandma always said the best way to solve a puzzle is to get your mind on something else. I tried to think about Mama, the way she smelled, the way her fingers felt, running up and down my back when I couldn't sleep. I pulled out Mama's paper and sniffed. It didn't exactly smell like Mama, but it was close—like violets and green things.

Every year on the first half-warm day of spring, Mama pulled me outside to look for violets. She poured the stems and flowers into a stew of shredded-up newspapers and threw in some dried rose petals she'd been saving since summer. She plucked an eyelash off each of us and threw them in the pot, too. She added a hair from Daddy's brush, lint from towel day, and whatever else struck her fancy. Mama didn't take the pot off the heat until the pulp was soft as lasagna noodles and all melted together. Then we spread it on an old window screen.

After the paper was dry, me and Mama would spend the whole day drawing still lifes of fruit and bird nests Mama set up for us.

Mama spent hours sitting across the table from me, drawing, but she never showed me her pictures. She said it was bad luck for her. She kept an arm curled around the side of her paper. When she was done, she rolled up each picture and piled them on the top shelf of her closet.

They disappeared when she did.

What was in those pictures that she wouldn't let me see?

Half of me was hating Mama for hiding her pictures, and the other half was hating me for hating Mama.

It wasn't her fault. That was just Mama's way. As soon as I proved the Bird Room was real, Mama wouldn't need to go off looking for birds anymore because I would have found them.

A little voice in my head said that maybe Mama wouldn't even show up at the cemetery. But I just huddled Daddy's jacket around me and tried to remember the rose-violet smell of Mama's paper when it was fresh and warm.

I dreamed about Mama's paper, that paper laid out forever, one long, blank page waiting for me and Mama to draw all new things.

Mama's paper was still unwinding in my head when the bird songs woke me up. It stayed with me all the way through my peanut butter breakfast, through building the fire back up, and through boiling my water.

The last time me and Mama used her paper was at our picnic near the cemetery in Columbus. We spent the afternoon making rubbings of carved angels from the headstones.

Then it hit me—I couldn't see what those marks on the cemetery rock were saying, but maybe I could take a rubbing.

I carried the rock to the creek and washed it off. I left it wet so Mama's paper would stick. I sharpened my pencil and, starting from one side, scraped the lead across the paper on the stone.

Shapes started showing—the lines of a feather.

And below it, what could have been a line of writing. But the letters didn't make sense.

Is this in some kind of foreign language?

The only thing I knew how to say in another language was *pantalones rojos,* and red pants weren't going to help me now.

Wait. The letters leaned to the left.

But don't most people slant their handwriting to the *right*?

Mama'd told me once how Leonardo da Vinci used backward writing. Maybe that's what this was.

But the way to read backward writing is by looking at it in a mirror.

And I sure didn't have a mirror out here.

Stupid woods.

Then I recollected what Grandma always said. "Where there's a will, there's a way."

Maybe I didn't need a mirror. Maybe all I needed to do was look at it backward.

But how?

I had an idea. My writing used to go through to the other side of the notebook paper if I pressed my pencil down too hard. Maybe I could look at the writing from the other side.

I went over those markings again and again with my pencil until they were thick and dark.

I turned the paper to the other side, but I still couldn't make out the words.

A song started playing through my head, one of Grandma's favorites: "Keep on the Sunny Side."

And that's how I knew Grandma was still helping.

I walked out to a clearing, turned over the paper, and held it up to the sun.

The words appeared.

LOOK LIKE A RABBIT GO
WHERE THE SHIMMERING STOPS

Everything tingled inside me. I'd found another one of Mr. Bob's clues!

But what did it mean?

CHAPTER 16

LOOKING LIKE A RABBIT

Mama started calling me Cricket when I was a baby. She said crickets bring happiness, and that's sure what I'd done, just by being born. Besides, she said, crickets are resourceful, and nobody else could make a staircase out of stuffed animals the way I did whenever I got the notion to climb out of my crib in the middle of the night.

Now I'd need every bit of that resourcefulness if I was going to figure out how to look like a rabbit.

"Okay," I told Charlene over our peanut-butter-and-clover breakfast. "Rabbits are gray and small and twitchy. How can I look like a rabbit, and why would anybody want me to?"

74

She twitched her antennae at me.

"Nice try." I smoothed her antennae back down. "But you're not no rabbit."

I put her back in her box and started walking the sidewalks, looking for clues and food and trying to look like a rabbit, whatever that meant.

But the thing about not having the book is, you wonder what you're supposed to be doing. What you'd be doing if you knew better.

It was like the homeschooling time with Mama all over again. Even *I* knew we were supposed to be keeping to some kind of schedule. After Daddy told me to keep an eye on Mama and headed offshore, it was all I could do to talk her into getting dressed before lunchtime. We'd start out aiming to cover adverbs or tectonic plates, and I'd end up getting put on "independent study" with a library book while Mama drew picture after picture, her free arm wrapped tight around each one.

After all that walking, all morning long, all I managed to do was lose the bright-green top button off Daddy's jacket and stir up a bunny who jumped away, fast as I saw him.

I retraced my steps back to the tree house, but that button was gone. It felt like I'd lost a little piece of Daddy.

Charlene started up chirping. At least I still had her. I gave her a little bit of peanut butter, but she still kept calling.

When I got ready to set out again, Charlene hopped right up on my shoulder.

"You want to come?"

She turned those puppy-dog brown eyes of hers on me and let out a slow, soft chirp.

Having Charlene out there with me, I felt like she was guiding me. When Charlene looked just the slightest bit to the left, I went with it.

Turns out, Charlene was a genius at finding food.

Not so much with clues.

Charlene steered me past what used to be a rose trellis, the vines all thorny and tangled, past the street with spread-out columns where the front offices used to be. When we came to a place where the weeds were pushed to the side, we saw faint prints in the dirt. Charlene stared at the trail. I followed and, just around a bend, saw whatever made those prints must have been eating from—a field of clover, dandelion greens, wild onion, and two hickory-nut trees. I gathered up as much as I could carry.

My brain had two sharp edges now, but only one of them was happy. The finding-food-and-keeping-warm part was ready to celebrate. Our fire was going strong, and my coat pockets were filled with hickory nuts and greens. But

76

the other edge, the solving-the-puzzle part, was itchy and mad. We'd covered a lot of ground but hadn't found anything shimmering.

And I wasn't even one step closer to figuring out how to look like a rabbit.

I'd run out of ideas. I needed to get my mind on something else. Plus, I was starving.

I needed to do something I at least halfway knew how to do.

I remembered Mama teaching me how to make green-onion pancakes to fold around chopped-up pecans. Even if it lasted for just one second, I wanted the woods to smell like Mama's kitchen. "Let's make pancakes for lunch," I told Charlene.

I made a mash out of dandelion greens, wild onions, and a dab of peanut butter, spread it on the pan with some oil from the peanut butter for grease, and let my fire sizzle it up.

I skimmed off the pancake with the point of my pocket knife and folded it around the hickory-nut pieces and peanut butter—more protein to help me make it the nine days till Mama.

I shared the woods burrito with Charlene. "You've earned a big piece. If we hadn't followed that animal trail you spotted, we never would have gotten all this food."

Charlene started chirping up a storm.

That was it!

Maybe the clue didn't mean that I should make myself look like a rabbit. Maybe it meant that I should look at things the way a rabbit would.

Rabbits stay close to the ground—like on that trail we'd followed. Maybe rabbits had even made the trail.

And what had Daddy told me about rabbits?

They burrow in the dirt. They keep their babies underground.

Like a buried surprise.

"The buried surprise Mr. Bob promised!" I hollered. "That's what the clue means. All we need now is to find where the shimmering stops and dig there."

My mind started galloping.

Where would I find something shimmering in a town where everything was crumbling apart?

CHAPTER 17

UNRAVELING THE KNOT

Grandma always said to unravel the knot from the loose end. Start from the beginning. Me and Charlene hurried to the sign at the edge of town, the sign that announced the start of Electric City.

Block by block, we walked the woods, my hand shovel in my back pocket, looking for anything shimmery. Maybe there were some old windows. Would those count as shimmery?

Nothing, not even close, all afternoon.

Was this how Mama felt all those years—looking for the Bird Room but not finding it?

The sun slanted its red warning-sign light at me. It was

getting late. Still, I couldn't give up yet. I passed Daddy's old homeplace, the library site, the empty, sunk-in spot where the theater used to be.

Charlene started twitching her antennae to the right.

Then I saw them: quartz rocks lining each side of the sidewalk leading to the theater. The orange-red light glinted off each shiny, shimmery edge.

CHAPTER 18

WRONG WALLS

Starting where the theater sidewalk ended, I got to digging, fast as I could.

My shovel struck something hard—a metal lunch box, the old-timey kind.

I let out a whoop. We'd solved it! We'd found the buried surprise!

Inside, there was a heavy, square wooden box made out of two different kinds of wood—a dark wood on the bottom and a light wood on the top. A circle was carved into the top of the box, near the edge. A special kind of box for a special kind of surprise.

I went to open it. The light part seemed like it should be the lid, but there wasn't a handle.

I tried the lid. Stuck.

Not even my pocketknife could pry it open.

Maybe after all those years of being buried in the cold dirt, something had gummed it up. I headed back to the tree house, got the fire going good, and hugged the box in my lap, letting it warm up.

I tried again to jimmy the lid loose.

If anything, the heat just made it tighter.

Should I smash the box with some rocks? But that might break whatever was inside.

I was this close to Mama's surprise, and the lid wouldn't budge, not one single, tiny bit.

"You try." I showed Charlene the box.

She jumped on it and started tapping her way across the top. She stumbled on the carved circle.

I should have seen it before—in the middle of the circle was a shallow carving, a little upside-down balloon with its blowing end chopped off and the knot missing.

Why would that Bob guy put a carving of a balloon on a box that didn't open?

That carving had to mean something.

I closed my eyes and pretended Mama was right there beside me, pointing out things to notice.

I'd seen something shaped like that before. I just needed to remember what.

I thought about all those cartoons where a lightbulb goes on over somebody's head when they figure something out. I wanted a lightbulb moment, too.

And then, that's exactly what I got.

Because I remembered the lightbulb carved in the middle of my doogaloo.

The doogaloo that looked to be exactly the size of that circle.

I grabbed the coin off the clue shelf.

Soon as I put it in the circle, something inside the box clicked.

When I tried the box again, the top slid off.

Inside, there was a piece of paper with a drawing of a tanager. The tanager reminded me of the tanager that used to be on my doogaloo.

Just below the tanager, slanty words:

SOME WALLS AREN'T FOR EVERYONE

My whole body drooped. This wasn't Mama's surprise.

And it was like that Bob person didn't want anyone to solve the clue trail.

CHAPTER 19

SPIDERWEBS

Some walls aren't for everyone. That line played in my head all night. But the second my eyes snapped open, I saw me and Charlene had bigger things to worry about.

The clouded-up sky looked like eraser smudges on worn-out paper. White frost covered the leaves. Hundreds of spiderwebs hunkered just off the ground, in every low bush.

Something had spooked all the spiders. Spooked them bad enough to make them cluster up close.

No bird sounds. Just bare branches scraping in the wind.

Icy air hit my skin.

A storm was headed for our woods.

I scurried down the ladder and threw more logs on the fire to keep it going.

A crinkling sound came toward us.

Then I felt the sleet.

I snatched up as much dandelion and rye grass for me and Charlene as I could, grabbed the hot stones from the fire with the edge of Daddy's jacket, and ran for the tree house.

The ice beat up against the shutters.

Charlene twitched her antennae at me, nervous-like. Had she ever been through a storm?

She crawled deep inside my sleeve. Pulling my knees tight, I poured my breath in to her. It became a warm white cloud, something for Charlene to hold on to.

Charlene was brave. She stayed steady, her antennae down, tapping my arm every so often.

Breathe in. Breathe out.

I tried to picture the rest of the world going about its business. Keisha getting up in Mobile, wondering if her school would be closed. My cousins making sleet balls to throw at each other. Aunt Belinda setting out mugs for hot chocolate.

Outside, the light turned blurry.

A tree limb crashed.

What if a limb knocks the tree house loose from the tree?

Some walls aren't for everyone. Maybe it wasn't a clue. Maybe it was a warning.

I didn't belong in these woods.

I stared at my clue shelf. How was I going to fill it now?

Me and Charlene nibbled at the peanut butter and hickory nuts, trying to make them last.

Why hadn't I gathered more food?

All the food I'd eaten in my life without really enjoying it, all the food I'd let go to waste, it paraded through my head, one bite after another. Mama's homemade chicken and dumplings, deviled eggs, deviled ham, hamburgers from Briggs Five Points, Aunt Belinda's Tater Tots casserole, cranberry sauce and turkey, tuna salad, s'mores, strawberry flapjacks, Frosted Flakes, and french fries. Even Grandma's brussels sprouts.

The cold got worse. I missed everything warm about my mama.

Not even those times she went away could change that. Days of me not knowing where she was, not knowing how to answer Grandma's questions. When she got back, Mama would just say, "Don't worry, Cricket. Everything's okay."

And then, with Mama back, it was.

One day, Mama took me with her. She crumpled up my homeschool worksheet, grabbed a pack of Big Red gum, jangled her keys at me, and dropped a fresh gardenia bloom on my desk. "Gardenias are like happiness," Mama said. "You get right up on it, and it doesn't smell like much. But if you step back and let it spread around the room, then you're on to something. Let's step back. Let's explore."

She drove all the way to Jackson without stopping once. We made a game of the trip, looking at all the houses, guessing who lived inside, how the rooms were laid out, what the people hung on their walls. It felt like magic passing by the Millsaps bell tower and being in that city with its tall buildings and murals and sculptures. It was so different from anything in Deerfield.

Mama screeched her car to a stop in front of the Mississippi Museum of Art. The way Mama bowed and held the door open for me, she made me feel like the whole museum was set up just for me.

I followed Mama as she flitted from one picture to another, lingering over only one painting, *The Garden Steps*. "Pay attention, Cricket," Mama said. "Feel the music from the picture."

She leaned up against the PLEASE DON'T TOUCH THE ARTWORK sign and ran her fingers over the canvas. "I remember the music from the Bird Room. When I peeked through that keyhole, I saw a whole room singing and dancing." She touched my shoulder but kept her eyes on that painting. "A room that held the whole outdoors."

Mama turned to me, her face lit up.

"You're an artist, Cricket. Don't you forget that."

Before we could see even half of the exhibits, the museum guard and his sneak-up-on-you shoes appeared.

"We're closing, ladies. Please finish your tour."

I pulled Mama toward the door, but we both couldn't help stopping for a minute over an engraving of birds by an artist named John James Audubon. "This place is beautiful, Mama. I reckon it has about everything there is to see in the whole state."

Mama put her fingers to her lips. "There's something missing."

Mama spit out her gum, opened her purse, pulled out a drawing of a bird's nest I'd done the week before, and stuck it to the glass over the engraving.

She smoothed out the wrinkles. "There. Much better. Finest in the whole museum." Mama gathered me in a hug.

The guard was heading back our way. I hustled Mama out to the car.

On the way home, we ran out of gas and had to walk a mile to the gas station. When we got there, Mama flirted with a convertible driver in a cowboy hat to get us a ride back to our car, a scary trip with him driving too fast and looking over at Mama the whole way.

None of that mattered one bit.

I was safe with Mama. She liked my picture best.

But now in the tree house, the cold seeped in at me and

Charlene. I squeezed my eyes shut and tried to bring back the smell of Mama's gardenia.

I thought about how lonely it must have been for Mama, off looking for the Bird Room by herself all these years. Never finding it. Why didn't she just give up?

Then I knew.

The way Grandma always asked Mama a question and looked at me to see if Mama was telling the whole truth. The way Grandma always went behind Mama's back, always snooping in the medicine cabinet, even after that time Mama filled it with marbles. The way even Daddy had started to treat her different toward the end. Who could Mama feel safe with?

And the Bird Room was the beginning of all that.

If Mama could prove the Bird Room was real, she'd prove she wasn't crazy.

After all these years of not finding it, had Mama started to doubt? Maybe she needed to prove something to herself, too.

I woke up the next morning with Charlene crawling on my shoulder and the sun sparkling from a thousand icy shards.

But our tree house was still nailed tight against the tree.

All around us, there were broken-off branches.

It was funny, though.

The few trees with high branches still on them had squirrel nests in those branches.

I craned my neck. The same old tight lump of squirrel-nest leaves still hung ten feet above us.

The squirrels bet on my and Charlene's tree.

The squirrels bet on us.

CHAPTER 20

CLUE-SEARCHING WEATHER

From the bright of my rebuilt fire, the woods looked even emptier. Every branch, every leaf, every twig, was trapped inside a thick layer of ice. Nothing green, just rust-colored honeysuckle vines.

My too-fast breath puffed little white clouds in the empty air.

The woods hadn't taught me anything that could help us in this kind of weather. The peanut butter wouldn't last.

How will I find more food?

I had to. That was all there was to it.

Charlene was counting on me.

And Mama would be here in a week.

I tromped through the woods. The ice was melting, leaving behind mud and limp, leaned-over greens. Even after I washed them in the cold creek water, they tasted mostly like grit.

The water rippled.

A fish was striking at something. A fish!

Maybe the woods had taught me this one big thing—you do what you have to do.

But I didn't have a hook to go fishing the regular way.

The book! I scampered back to the tree house, picked up what was left of the book, and learned up on how to make fish traps. I read the directions twice to make sure I had everything right. Then I gathered supplies—honeysuckle vines, lots of sticks, and the wire from the tree house. I peeled the bark off the honeysuckle to make rope and imagined the way Daddy would do it, sure and steady. I made a cone out of sticks and honeysuckle rope and put it inside a sort of barrel kind of thing I made from more sticks, honeysuckle rope, and wire. That way, the fish would swim through the cone to get the bait but wouldn't be able to find their way out.

I smeared a little gob of peanut butter on the inside of the cone to bait the trap. Then I sank it where I'd seen the flicker of fins.

The whole thing held together. I'd done it! The first big thing I'd ever built all by myself.

＊ ＊ ＊

When the trap finally worked, I almost wished it hadn't. The sight of that hopeful fish near about made my legs go out from under me.

But I cleaned it the way the book showed me and fried it up in peanut butter juice.

Its smoky flavor hit my tongue, and I'd never tasted anything so good. I could even taste the hickory flavor from some wood I'd used for the fire.

Still, I couldn't enjoy it all the way. Soon as supper was over, me and Charlene had a little funeral for what was left of the fish. "I hope you lived a happy life. Thank you for providing for us."

I thought about all the fish I'd eaten at the fry, around Mama's table, and even at Aunt Belinda's. I'd never once thought to thank the fish. This time felt different. It was personal between me and that fish.

A coyote yipped from somewhere far off.

"No coyote would ever have a funeral for a fish," I told Charlene.

She didn't look at me.

But the fish gave me enough energy to keep looking for clues and bring back Charlene a good mess of chickweed. So we were both getting fed, and that had to be a good thing, didn't it?

*** * ***

It was weird, but after I'd spent so much time outside, my every sense felt sharper. I felt like a part of the woods now, even if I *was* a part that was eating up some of the other parts. I noticed things more. I could taste things and smell things better. It even felt like I could think things quicker.

By afternoon, it had warmed up into clue-searching weather.

My eyes darted around the homeplaces, looking for walls and tanagers.

I swung on a possum grapevine hanging from a big tree, that question thumping through my head: *What walls aren't for everyone?*

Could there be a house or barn near whatever was putting out that hickory smoke?

No. Mama said the Bird Room house was in a big, nice neighborhood, not out in the middle of nowhere. Besides, there's lots of hunters out this time of year. It was probably one of their campfires I smelled.

I swung that possum grapevine higher, giving me a little better view. Lots of homeplaces I hadn't combed all the way through yet.

I'd made it through the ice storm, and I was feeding myself from the woods. I'd found the feather rock. I'd found the tanager tree. I'd figured out how to open the wood box. If there was another basement wall out here, I was sure going to find it.

Grandma would help.

"Charlene," I said, "we're in the home stretch now."

CHAPTER 21

PERCY

I felt the bite before I saw the snake. Another warmish day, and I was out looking for basements with the doogaloo in my pocket for luck.

I should have known better than to walk too near those rocks. Charlene was on my shoulder, and even she didn't see it coming.

Pain shot through my left ankle.

It felt like I'd just touched the prong of a half-plugged-in lamp cord.

I lurched back.

The snake coiled fat and low.

Those yellow eyes didn't show one speck of mercy. An

hourglass pattern stretched down his pink-brown back. He wiggled his tail, but there wasn't a rattle. His overripe cucumber smell hit my nose, and I knew.

Copperhead.

I'd heard Daddy tell stories about that smell. A bad-enough bite could kill you.

Everything went quiet except for the cicada heartbeat slamming in my ears.

From the east, I smelled more hickory smoke.

Was it friendly smoke or "turn you in" smoke?

It wasn't any time to start getting picky. To me, it looked like maybe "save your life" smoke.

Tucking Charlene in close, I ran, best as I could.

I went farther than I'd ever been.

The sidewalks stopped, and so did the briars. I kept going, past straight rows of trees, past a pond. Crows cackled and cawed above me.

The top of a two-story house appeared. Something was moving on the roof. Far off, I saw what looked to be a driveway.

Out of nowhere, a huge three-colored dog bounded up. His body swiveled back and forth, powered by the fastest-wagging tail I'd ever seen on a dog. He came to a dirt-cloud stop in front of me and dropped into a sit. He cocked his head, held out a huge paw, and bobbed it up and down.

Help. I just needed help. Where was his owner?

And why was he blocking my way?

But that tail was wagging, and that had to be a good sign. Right?

I shook the paw he was still wiggling at me.

He sprang up and led me toward the house, like he was getting ready to introduce me.

Something was still stirring around on that roof.

I could feel the skin on my ankle pulling as it swelled.

Everything was coming at me bugs-on-a-bike-ride fast.

Then I saw the lady. She was clomping up on the roof and swishing a mop. A tall ladder leaned up against the front of her house with its even-spaced windows. She started yelling churchgoing cuss words. "Heavens to Betsy! Tarnation! There's more up here that needs patching than I thought, Percy. What we really need is a new roof."

She came down the ladder, red-faced, and stopped at the bottom rung when she saw me.

For a second, we stared at each other.

She wore a cowboy hat with turned-down sides, a camouflage jacket, a long skirt, and black-specked sneakers. She nodded at me like she saw girls appear out of the woods every day of the week. "That's Percy. Don't let him think he's got your attention. He'll be impossible to live with." She smoothed back her hair. "Have you earned your survival badge yet, or do you need to go back and chop some more wood?"

Huh?

"Don't you know you can't break so much as a twig in these woods without the crows hearing it and letting me know? These birds only have me to keep track of. Young lady, you're some kind of exciting news to those crows. Why do you think they've been bringing me all this?" She pointed at a bird feeder covered in scattered peanut shells. There were two crawdad shells and my missing button.

"Ma'am, I need help."

A buzzing metal taste had took over my mouth. It felt like every mistake I'd ever made was right there on my tongue.

I slumped on the front steps, rolled up my pant leg, and pulled off my shoe and sock. The skin swelled up around two red holes.

The lady squatted down, ran two fingers over the bite, and clucked her tongue.

"He only got you once." She straightened. "You'll live. Come on in." She opened the front door.

I followed her inside and sank into the daybed she pointed to.

The lady grabbed hold of my hurt ankle. "Hang it off the side of the bed. Keep it lower than your heart. I'll be back in a jiffy." She disappeared behind a door.

Charlene huddled in my sleeve, smoothing her antennae against my arm.

Back in front of me now, the lady held a weighted-down dishrag.

She pulled out a gray stone about half the size of a hen's egg. "This here's a madstone."

Mama. I just want Mama.

She laid the hot, rough stone on my bite and circled the stone with her fingers.

"The best madstones, like this one, come out of white-furred deer. This one has cured both rabies and snakebites. Don't move."

What in the world is she talking about? Is this really happening?

The stone sucked at my skin until the rock went bathroom-tile cold.

The pain eased back a notch.

The lady let out a loud breath, trotted off, and came back with a bowl full of milk, steam rising off the top. "Watch." Using the dishrag, she lifted the stone and slid it into the bowl.

Green lines swiggled out of that stone and marbled the top of the milk. After a couple of minutes, the whole bowl was covered in a foamy green scum.

She ran her fingers over my ankle and nodded. "I got most of that venom out. You rest now." She hurried up a narrow staircase in the corner and came down carrying a box full of jars with masking-tape labels.

She plucked out a jar. "Wild plantain." She scooped out a bunch of chopped black bits, spread the lumpy mix on my ankle, and wrapped a dish towel around it. Then she handed me a coffee cup filled with something that smelled the way jelly does if it's sat out on the counter too long. "Drink this. It'll help you sleep."

Holding my nose, I drank it down.

My eyelids scratched, sandy, against my eyes.

Every part of me was giving in.

Using my last awake breath, I eased Charlene out of my sleeve. "Can you take care of her for me?"

The lady didn't snatch Charlene up the way I thought she would. Instead, she held her palm out flat like a bridge. She kept it still and steady while Charlene tapped her way across it, one lacy leg at a time.

CHAPTER 22

THE MAMA BIRD

They say that when you're dying, your whole life flashes before your eyes.

But it wasn't my whole life that I saw.

All that I saw, over and over, was my last Christmas tree with Mama and Daddy.

I was studying up on homeschool pre-algebra and Daddy was frying wild turkey breast for dinner when Mama banged open the back door, her eyes sparkling. "I've found our tree."

Mama walked fast, inventing her own route. We followed her past the waterfall me and Mama had built out of rocks in the stream, past the pecan grove, deep into the woods.

Mama's tree was a cedar, the dark-green color of Christmas.

As soon as Daddy put the tree in the base and set it in the living room, Mama pulled out six boxes of lights. "Let's do them close. You know I like them close."

We strung the lights, two strands to a limb, until the light filled the whole living room.

Mama pulled out a box labeled *Fragile* in Grandma's handwriting. I'd only seen the box once, when Grandma showed me the handblown glass ornaments she'd gotten from *her* grandma in Germany.

"I don't think we should . . . ," I said, but Mama was already unwrapping thin glass shapes—clocks, smiling babies, happy couples. But the best, the most beautiful, was the gold angel with green eyes like Mama's.

"When I was your age, your grandma wouldn't even let me in the same room with this angel, it's so old. She said to keep this one put away." Mama traced her fingers down the ornament. "But what's the point of having pretty things if you can't enjoy them?"

Mama hung that angel next to the glitter-spackled sweet-gum ball ornaments I'd made when I was four.

The next night, Daddy had to go to a Lions Club meeting. On his way out the front door, he shot me a look. "Keep an eye on your mama," he said. "She's been staring at that tree for hours and is back to pacing again."

Daddy's truck had just left the driveway when I heard Mama yelling, "Cricket, come here quick." Mama pointed to a bird's nest made of twigs, bark strips, grass, and threads. It was so deep inside the tree that you'd never see it if you weren't looking hard. The nest was woven tight, with a tiny blue thread going through the side. That thread made so many zigs and zags that it almost looked like writing.

Mama hugged my arm around her waist and eased out the blue thread. "This looks like it came from your jacket."

She studied the thread and balled it up into a tight bead. "You know what I think happened, baby? That mama bird gathered up every pretty thing she could find for that nest. She guarded that egg. She fed the baby bird all the food she could find. Till one day, that baby bird spread its wings and that mama bird knew, she just knew, that baby could fly."

Eyes still on the tree, Mama handed me that string. "Then that mother bird got out of the way and she let that baby bird fly off." Mama looked out the window. "That bird is probably floating on a breeze right this minute over our house. I bet that baby just soared. Just like you'll do when you're a famous artist."

My eyes cut to the window, but it was too dark outside to see.

Mama unhooked Grandma's angel ornament and propped it in the bird's nest. Not reclining, exactly. Just leaning up against the side of the nest, keeping an eye on things.

Carefully, I put the little ball of string next to the angel.

"No." Mama pressed it in my palm. "It's for you. For good luck."

"Thanks, Mama."

But Mama wasn't listening. She started back to pacing too fast. "First, I'm going to find me that Bird Room. Then I'm going to see that headstone put up proper, and then I'm going to . . ."

A familiar fear gripped me hard.

Mama's voice sounded the way it did that last time before she went into the hospital. "Mama, slow down."

She didn't even lift her eyes from the floorboards. She followed one straight line all the way to the window, whirled on her heels, and started over.

"Mama, you're scaring me."

She reached out a hand and brushed my cheek, but she didn't stop. "I've got to find the Bird Room," she said.

"Look at the tree, Mama." I pulled her down so we lay side by side under the branches. I pointed into the lit-up limbs. "See how pretty."

Mama's ankle wrapped around mine in a hug, but her foot didn't stop tapping. I stared up into the blinking lights for the longest time, soaking up that cedar smell and trying to soothe some of that cedar calm into Mama.

She started singing "Ring of Fire," off key and too fast.

"No, Mama, sing something else." I started up humming "Jingle Bells."

Mama just sang faster, the way she sang last time before she needed to go to the hospital and I had to stay at Aunt Belinda's while Daddy was offshore. Me and my homeschool books, trying to make up for lost time and getting behind. I mailed a card every day to Mama but never got a single one back, and she wouldn't even talk to me on the phone, and all Aunt Belinda did was say, "Be patient and your mama will be home soon," and people looked at me funny and asked me questions I couldn't answer. I hated it, every single bit of it, and here she was, acting that way again.

She was worse than a mama bird about to fly off and leave its half-feathered baby behind.

The words flew out of my mouth. "Stop it! Rooms aren't alive. I wish you'd just be normal."

Mama's foot stopped tapping. She turned toward me. Her eyes were dark mud puddles of hurt.

Mama's face crumpled with cry sounds that didn't make it past her lips.

"No, Mama, I didn't mean it."

But she already had her back to me.

When she finally spoke, her voice was a chalky whisper. "Me too."

From her perch in the bird's nest, the angel ornament stared at me. She heard everything.

Mama scrambled up, went to her bedroom, and clicked the lock shut.

I couldn't believe what I'd just said to my mama. The mama who built me waterfalls, who read me poetry, the mama who called me an artist, the mama who took me places no one else would ever think to go.

I'd just told her I wished she was somebody else.

CHAPTER 23

GONE

My words were sour in my mouth as I stood outside Mama's door. "Mama, I didn't mean it," I said again.

But she wouldn't open the door.

When Daddy got home, I didn't say one word to him. He'd make things better like he always did. He'd get Mama back on her medicine, and we'd forget about that night, just the way we forgot about everything else bad.

Still, I couldn't sleep. All I could see was the hurt in Mama's eyes. I lay in bed and listened to the heat cycling on and off, on and off.

When I woke up, the house felt hollow.

Daddy slouched over the kitchen table, stirring his

coffee with a worn-out spoon. But I knew good and well he always took his coffee black.

"Where's Mama?" I asked.

He didn't look up. He just shook his head.

Mama's cell phone lay on the table beside him. Her purse and keys were missing from their hook on the wall.

I ran to their bedroom. Her underwear drawer was sticking out, half-empty. The suitcase, the one we used that time we went to Biloxi, it was missing, too.

So were the rolled-up drawings.

And her favorite nightgown, the silky one with blue roses.

Gone.

It was all my fault.

I pulled open the rest of the dresser drawers.

Mostly full.

I ran back into the kitchen. "Look, Daddy," I said. "She didn't take much. She'll be back soon."

"I'm sure she will, honey," he said. "Here, let me fix you breakfast." He scrambled some eggs and sat there while I pushed the food around my plate.

"When your mama gets back, we'll buy three more strings of lights for that tree." He forced his lips into a smile.

"That sounds good, Daddy."

I wanted to hug him, but Daddy wasn't all huggy like Mama.

He got up to clear the plate.

I shot up out of my chair. "No, Daddy, let me."

Mama's green aventurine ring lay in a gob of dried-out hand soap beside the sink.

The ring Daddy gave her the day I was born.

The ring that had been handed down in Daddy's family from Great-Aunt Lillian, who swore it brought her good luck every day of her life. The ring my mama never took off.

Left on the edge of the kitchen sink where anybody could have knocked it down the drain.

I held it up so Daddy could see.

He gathered me into a hug, leaning his stubbly chin into the top of my head.

Neither one of us let go until the phone rang—somebody looking for Mama.

After that, I woke up every morning to no sign of Mama and the floor beside the tree littered with more needles and ornaments the tree had shrugged off in the night.

That tree was dying, and it didn't matter how much water I poured in the base.

The angel was the last of the ornaments to fall.

I found her shattered on the floor, one eye staring up into the tree.

I swept up the pieces and buried them, dustpan and all, in the deepest hole I could dig in the yellow clay behind the barn.

Mama was gone, and there wasn't one single thing I could do about it.

Now I lay in a dark daybed in a stranger's house. I tried to get that angel out of my head.

I couldn't do it.

But my brain *did* bring up one word. It pierced through everything, sharp as sunlight through ice: *Tanager.*

I could change things with Mama if I could just live through this first.

CHAPTER 24

RIDDLES

Flannel. I was wearing somebody's flannel nightgown.

My ankle burned. I was so tired, I felt like a mashed bug, but I was more awake than I'd ever been.

Plus, I was hearing voices.

The living room was empty except for Charlene. She sat in a little cage that looked like it had last held a canary, with a thimble of water and a slice of sweet potato beside her.

The sound was coming from outside.

Okay, maybe it was just one voice.

But it was schoolteacher loud.

I parted the curtain. It was that lady talking. She held out three books to Percy. His tail was wagging for all get-out.

He sat, lifted a clown-shoe-size paw, and scratched at the middle book.

She commenced to reading. " 'Hope' is the thing with feathers," she announced. "By your favorite poet.

> " 'Hope' is the thing with feathers—
> That perches in the soul—
> And sings the tune without the words—
> And never stops—at all."

She went on, but I wasn't listening. I knew that poem. Mama used to recite the first line whenever she saw a cardinal. And why was that lady reading my mama's favorite poem to a *dog*?

Soon as the poem was over, Percy held out his paw for the lady to shake, jumped up, ran over to the edge of the garden, and dug five holes, one right beside the other.

What kind of place am I in?

The lady walked inside and slid the book back on the shelf. If her face and tied-back gray hair were any clues, she must have been at least seventy years old, but she didn't have that old-person, overripe tomato smell. She smelled more like hickory smoke and black pepper. Her eyes were as bright and brown as a rabbit's. Plus, she had the straightest posture I'd ever seen, even better than Grandma's.

She looked over my way and gave a little jump. She

probably thought I'd still be asleep. And she must've seen my expression. "Guess you heard that."

"Emily Dickinson."

I swear, that lady looked like I'd just said a secret password. Her face lit up. Then her expression got serious. She pointed toward Percy, out in the yard. "Let's just keep all the rest between ourselves, now, shall we?"

"Yes, ma'am."

Shoot. I'm a pro at keeping my mouth shut. I knew how to hold things so close, I didn't even say them to myself. Mama's pills, the schoolwork we were supposed to be doing, Mama flirting with any man wearing the right kind of cowboy hat.

"So . . . Percy likes poetry. I never met a dog like that before."

"Oh, it helps calm him down. That Percy, he's got quite the particular taste. He's a big fan of our friend Emily. And Langston Hughes and Walt Whitman. But he near about bit the book out of my hand when I tried to read him some E. E. Cummings." She stopped. "I'm forgetting my manners. My name's Vidalia. You can call me Miss V. You've been sleeping a day and a half."

"I'm Cricket." I pushed out the words.

Soon as I did it, I knew I'd messed up. I should have told her a fake name in case she'd heard about me running off.

Miss V. just nodded. That name didn't seem to mean

anything to her. "You know, you're the first person I've talked to in years who recognized that poem. I'm going to call you Ace."

She glanced out the window. "We ought to call your parents and let them know you're okay." She reached for the phone.

I rubbed at my ankle to buy myself some time.

"Ma'am, I sure do wish we could reach them, but they're on a cruise to Alaska. Won't be back for a week."

"Mm-hmm." By her face, I couldn't tell if she believed me or not.

I tried to look innocent.

She watched me for a minute. "Well, let's get you fed, then." She propped me up on the pillows and disappeared into the kitchen.

When she came back, I got a whiff of the pure delicious-ness wafting off the plate on the tray she was carrying. The tray held enough bacon and fried eggs to choke a horse.

The bacon half crumbled, half melted on my tongue. It was the best breakfast I'd had since Daddy died. And not just because I was starving. Skillet-fried bacon makes me feel like the day might turn out right.

It felt like a miracle to eat food I hadn't had to forage for and to be warm without having to hunt for branches for a fire.

I looked up. Miss V. was still standing there, waiting on

me to finish. "I'm much obliged," I said, trying to take the same tone Grandma used when a stranger gave her directions. "I hope I can repay you for your trouble."

Miss V. studied me, careful-like. "How are you at riddles?"

I hadn't so much as heard a riddle since second grade. "The best."

"I have a riddle for you to solve. What's only one color but not one size, stuck at the bottom, yet easily flies?"

I shrugged up empty hands.

She smoothed a wrinkle out of her shirt. "No matter. I just wondered if you knew it. You can think about it later." She looked at her watch. "Why don't you come outside and keep me company? The outdoor air will do you good." She reached behind her and handed me a pile of my clean and folded clothes.

I tested my ankle. The skin over it had turned the grainy brown color of a used-up tea bag. It still hurt some, but the swelling was down, and it could bear weight.

I got dressed in her bathroom and followed her onto the porch. I sat in a rocking chair and propped up my hurt foot on the stool she'd dragged over.

Percy stopped his hole digging and did a little side wiggle toward me, trying to walk, wag his tail, and nibble at it at the same time. He wore a bright bull's-eye-red collar, and that was the only normal-dog thing about him. He had hang-down hound-dog ears, but they were cocked at the top like he was always listening, really hard. He stood as high as my waist, and his back legs looked like long, skinny rabbit legs. His eyes were the color of honeysuckle vines. Most of his body was black, but the inside of his legs was coon-dog tan, and he had a white skunk stripe from his chin to his chest.

"You rest," Miss V. said. She picked up a hatchet and chopped at some wood. "The roof's got a leak. I've been working on making tar out of pinewood and patching it. I should get back to it. The moon had a ring around it last night. Rain's coming. I need to keep that fire going and do more patching." She pointed to a campfire raging around an upside-down big black pot.

I tried to get my bearings.

This house was the only thing left standing anywhere near the woods where I'd found all those clues. Maybe Mama remembered wrong about the Bird Room house being in a big, nice neighborhood. This house was right by Electric City, and it had a driveway that Granddaddy could have driven to from the old town. Maybe the yard had a clue. Or the house. Or maybe the Bird Room was inside this very house.

I'd have to see if I could search it.

If I got on Miss V.'s good side, maybe I could find a way to look around. "Is there anything I can do to help?" I used my "yes, ma'am" voice.

"Tell you what. You watch the fire, make sure it doesn't run out of wood."

Percy came over. He sat, leaning into me, so close he rocked me back in my chair every time he wagged his tail.

That dog could put out some heat, and for the longest time, I just sat there, feeling his warm body next to mine and letting him rock me. I watched the fire and hollered to Miss V. when it got too low. I didn't say one word about a lady her age going up and down that ladder. And while I was watching the fire, I was watching the woods, looking for anything that might be another tanager tree, waiting for my chance to look around inside.

CHAPTER 25

STAR

It took me an hour to get my opening for clue hunting. On the porch, I practiced six different ways to look pitiful, and Miss V. finally shooed me back inside to rest.

But the living room didn't look like any kind of clue-hunting place. It looked like a cross between a library and Grandma's living room, the one she wouldn't let nobody but the preacher go in.

A flower-patterned couch was in talking distance to the daybed. Doilies were draped across everything, even the bookshelves. Books were everywhere, on tables and on a bookcase stretching across an entire wall. A black baby grand piano stood in one corner. The lid was down, and there was a doily on that, too. The staircase was in another corner. Some old, faded photos on the walls. Lots of plants.

From the roof came the sound of Miss V. swishing tar.

I tiptoed around, looking at every little thing. Not a single painting or carving.

Nothing tanager.

I thumbed through the shelf. There was book after book of poetry, just like Miss V.'d said, each of them with little paw scratch marks on the cover. There were books full of crossword puzzles, and other books, too—*Treasure Island* and *North Toward Home*. And dozens of dusty issues of *Mississippi Gardener's Almanac*.

I flipped through the books, but no tanager painting was hidden between the pages.

I crossed the hallway and peeked into the kitchen, into the dining room, the bathroom again, even into the bedroom.

No tanagers.

I'd covered all the rooms downstairs.

Outside the windows, there was just an ordinary garden and straight-rowed trees.

I started over, looking closer at the walls. The first thing hanging was a photo of Percy in a bow tie. The second was a photo of a man in paint-spattered clothes.

Suddenly, my ankle didn't hurt anymore, not even a tiny bit.

That man in the picture might be Mr. Bob.

I got Charlene out of her cage to help me look closer.

Together, we combed the room. Soon as we got near the piano, though, Charlene went just as wild as she did that day in the bathroom of Thelma's. She flitted from one doily to the next.

She finally landed on the piano lid, her back leg jutted out, stuck in that crocheted doily.

Gently, I eased the lid up to free her leg.

Charlene jumped on my shoulder and the doily slipped to the side. We both stared at what was inside the piano.

Stretched across the piano wires was something made out of metal and wood. I picked it up. Two straight metal rods swung from a thick, carved wood handle.

Why would anybody put *that* inside a piano?

Maybe it was some kind of tuning instrument.

My finger caught on something sharp.

A tiny tanager was carved into the wood base. It had a star in its mouth, smaller than a corn kernel.

And just below the star, marked so faint that at first I thought it was scratches:

WORTHY #2

CHAPTER 26

A DEEAL

'd found Worthy #2! A tanager clue was inside this very house!

That thought didn't have long to settle. Two seconds later, Miss V. strode in and slapped a rolled-up copy of the *Pickens County Messenger* on the coffee table. "It's a good thing Percy didn't chew up this one," she said. "Cruise, huh?"

A headline stretched across the entire front page.

SEARCH CONTINUES FOR PICKENS COUNTY GIRL

Working out of an operational headquarters at the Deerfield Fire Department, the search team continues their efforts to find Ariana "Cricket" Overland. No trace has been found of the missing girl.

"We're all just tore up about it," said Belinda Faye Overland, the missing girl's aunt. When asked about the possibility that Cricket might have run away, Ms. Overland said, "Cricket was very happy here. We took her in and treated her like a princess. She had everything she could ever want." When pressed for anything else out of the ordinary the day that Cricket disappeared, Ms. Overland reported that the delicious red velvet cake she'd just baked and sat outside her kitchen window to cool had disappeared, too. "I suspect foul play," she said.

Ms. Overland is working with her church on a bake sale to raise a reward for information leading to the safe return of Cricket. Concerned citizens are asked to send donations in care of the Deerfield Baptist Church. Pastor Dudley Limerick and his wife, Mary Beth, have led the congregation in raising more than $600.

"I just hope that we can get our girl back safe and sound," said Ms. Overland. In addition to helping to coordinate fund-raising efforts, Ms. Overland has begun spending evenings at the fire station to help cheer the team on.

Miss V. looked at me hard. "You've got the whole town worried."

My heart slumped clear down to my gut.

"I'll call the sheriff. He'll carry you back to town."

"You're turning me in?"

"You belong back with your family."

I was close enough to Mama to feel her coming, and I'd just found a tanager clue. Now here I was, about to lose everything. I opened my mouth to tell Miss V. I didn't have a family anymore, to tell her about Mama, to tell her about the headstone, to tell her about the tanager.

She thrust out her palm like a stop sign.

"If you knew why I left, you wouldn't send me back."

Her face showed that she didn't believe me.

"I've never heard of anybody who could heal a snakebite the way you did. Can't I stay here just a little bit longer and heal up all the way? Just two more days. Then I'll leave the next morning. I'll go back, I promise."

Miss V. let out a powerful sigh. "Lord knows I'm a sucker for a runaway. Sometimes resting up *can* help you sort things out. But do you really think two days will change things for you?"

"Yes, ma'am." I tried to sound like someone she could trust.

Her jaw tightened and eased, tightened and eased.

After forever, her eyes met mine again. "You can stay two more days, but you stay out of my business, and I'll stay out of yours. No snooping around."

"Yes, ma'am!"

The kitchen door swung shut behind her.

I'd done it. I'd bought myself a little time. *But why is Miss V. so worried about me snooping?*

My eyes went straight to that staircase. That was the only place I hadn't looked. Exactly what was up there that Miss V. didn't want me to see?

CHAPTER 27

SOMETHING WEIRD

We sat at Miss V.'s dining room table eating her fried fish, hush puppies, coleslaw, and homemade tartar sauce, me trying not to look antsy to look up those stairs.

All I could think about was Worthy #2.

Soon as we finished cleaning up, the rain started. The moon was bright when it peeked through the clouds, and thick slashes of raindrops showed through the windows.

The electricity flickered off.

Miss V. lit two kerosene lanterns and carried one to the living room. She didn't say anything, and neither did I. She opened the piano, did something I couldn't see with the tanager thing, and played a slow, quiet waltz. Percy howled along outside.

This had to be my chance. I pretended to fall asleep.

After a few minutes, Miss V. turned the lantern down low, tucked the blanket higher on my shoulders, and padded off to bed with the second lantern.

Her snores came quick.

Turning my lantern higher, I cocked my head at Charlene. She lit on me with those eyes of hers.

The rain would cover up any noise.

I crept toward the stairs.

The upstairs smelled of stirred-up dust with a sharp underbelly of Pine-Sol.

The staircase led straight into two large, connected rooms.

No paintings. No tanagers. Nothing but books and a beat-up suitcase.

I tiptoed through the rooms.

And stopped.

Something was weird.

Part of the upstairs was missing.

CHAPTER 28

MAMA'S TANAGER

The first room had eight windows—three on the back wall, two on the side wall, and three on the front wall. The second room had only four windows, three on the back wall and one on the side wall. The second room didn't have any windows on the front wall. Plus, that room was narrower than the first.

The second story of Miss V.'s house had six evenly spaced windows in front. I remembered that game me and Mama used to play, imagining how houses we passed would look on the inside. From what I saw here, the inside of Miss V.'s house didn't match the outside.

The second room should have eight windows, not four. Where were the other four windows?

A wall went across the place where the other windows should have been. That wall was bare except for one faded photo of a tulip.

The message from Mr. Bob flashed in my head. *Some walls aren't for everyone.*

I ran my hands over the wall, starting from the bottom and reaching as high as I could.

I felt for anything out of place.

Near the end of the wall, my fingers bumped into the tulip photo. I racked my brain. Had Mama said anything about a tulip?

Nothing I could remember. I kept moving across the wall. My finger hit a crack. It ran right under the middle of the picture frame.

I traced it—a door shape!

My thumb bumped against a keyhole. I looked in, and my heartbeat sped up.

Whatever was inside shined and shimmered. There must be moonlight coming from windows inside that room.

Two ducks, painted on the wall, stared back at me.

I stuck my finger in the keyhole and tried to pry it open.

Locked.

When I put my eye to the keyhole again, the light had shifted. The duck eyes were shadowed now. A tree with orange leaves glistened in the moonlight. A red bird with black feathers perched on a tree limb.

Mama's tanager!

CHAPTER 29

SOME WALLS AREN'T FOR EVERYONE

Quiet as I could, I tried the door again. The photo over the door rattled loose. Catching it, my fingers brushed something. Two somethings.

I turned it over. A postcard painting of two ducks was taped to the back. Those ducks looked kin to the ducks I'd just seen inside the room.

Then I felt the other thing, and for a second, I couldn't draw a clear breath. A key was tied to a blue ribbon—a key about the size of the lock on Mama's Bird Room.

I turned the key in the lock and eased the door open.

A soft heartbeat sound came from inside the narrow room.

Four painted-over windows bounced the moonlight around among themselves.

A black-capped chickadee, tail flicked up, perched on the branch of a pin oak. Curvy lines stretched out around the chickadee like question marks.

A miniature pond rose from the baseboard and blended into the floor. A bass hovered, midjump, closing in on a dragonfly. The moonlight flickered across the fish and made its scales glisten.

Freshly turned rows from Miss V.'s garden lined part of the walls. Honeysuckle vines hung from the bushes beside the garden.

Each wall looked like it was painted in a different season from Miss V.'s garden—winter, spring, summer, fall. You could tell by the trees.

Every little plant, every twig, every animal, had a rhythm.

Sparrows, cardinals, warblers, woodpeckers, doves, and crows wove through the branches.

The walls seemed to reach out and catch hold of me, whispering in my ear and singing.

This was the music my mama had heard.

Mama was right—the room *did* feel alive.

Every wall but the summer one had tanagers—flying in the garden or perched in trees. They were bright red on the spring wall and just starting to turn green on the fall wall. On the winter wall a huge green tanager caught my eye.

Just a minute. Something isn't right. The tanager doesn't belong on the winter wall.

Tanagers have already migrated by winter. No tanager would be in Miss V.'s woods then.

That clue—*Some walls aren't for everyone*—flashed in my head and itched its way around.

Maybe it wasn't a dead end. Maybe it was trying to tell me something.

But what?

The winter tanager was bigger than the others. That had to mean something, right?

Then I saw the knothole it was sitting on.

Red rings were painted around it. The same exact color as Percy's collar. Bull's-eye red. Those rings looked like circles around a target.

There had to be something in that hole. I poked in my finger.

It touched a dusty, waxy string. I pulled.

A yellow, rolled-up piece of paper crinkled out of the hole, tied together with the string.

I untied it and drew the lantern closer.

The note was dated the same day as Mama's birthday.

March 6, 1984

I'M HEADING HOME. THIS PLACE COULDN'T

CHANGE ME. THERE'S SOME THINGS YOU JUST

CAN'T CHANGE. BEHOLD YOUR WORLD.

I'VE BURIED A TREASURE FOR WHOEVER CAN

FOLLOW THE LIGHT TO FIND IT.

Love,
BOB

A treasure! The surprise he had told Mama about.

Below the words was a tiny trail of bird tracks down the page. So many, it looked like a whole bird convention.

Those tracks brought to mind the blue thread I'd seen in the nest in our Christmas tree. But why?

The lantern flickered, and I knew. The blue thread had

looked like writing in the bird's nest! I studied the note closer.

That's when I saw them—sideways letters in the tracks, spelling out these words:

START WITH THE TREASURE IN THIS HOUSE

CHAPTER 30

QUESTIONS

Those words hadn't even settled in my head before I heard another of those heartbeat sounds. I shined my light where it had come from—near the corner window.

A raindrop dripped into a half-full bucket. The ceiling above it was missing big flakes of paint and plaster.

The leak in the roof was tearing up this room!

Outside, a coyote howled. Percy started barking. He was liable to wake up Miss V. I retied the note and jammed it back in the hole so she wouldn't know I'd been up here.

Back on the daybed, questions flew at me, fast as moths against window glass.

Why would Miss V. hide that room?

Who was that Bob person who'd painted the room?

What about him couldn't be changed?

Why did he hide a treasure?

And what inside this house was the treasure I should start with?

CHAPTER 31

JUST MORE COLORFUL

When I woke up the next morning, even the light outside looked different. It was brighter and greener, and the air coming through Miss V.'s propped-open porch door smelled of every fresh new thing the rain had sprouted. I'd found Mama's room. I'd been inside it, even. Aunt Belinda's double-wide, with its dollar-store art hanging on the walls, seemed a million miles away. I'd stood where Mama'd stood. And I had another clue toward Mama's surprise.

I peeked around. No sign of Miss V. except for two ham biscuits she'd left for me on a napkin, next to the daybed.

Me and Charlene, we got to looking for clues.

We turned over every pillow, prodded into every crack in the baseboards, and felt for any more fake walls.

I was just about to turn over the photograph of Mr. Bob to look on the back when the door opened.

Miss V. handed me a copy of the *Messenger,* holding it by the corners, like she didn't want to touch it.

I was still front-page news.

NO CLUES IN MISSING-GIRL CASE

The search continues for Ariana "Cricket" Overland, who disappeared from the Deerfield community. No progress has been made.

The disappearance is the latest in a string of misfortunes for the family. Cricket's father died earlier this year. Her mother abandoned the family. Efforts to relocate her mother have been unsuccessful so far. According to two neighbors, her mother reportedly has a long history of mental issues and instability. Ms. Overland, Cricket's aunt, vigorously denied that report, however, stating that "she's no worse than anybody else walking around Pickens County. She's just more colorful."

The story went on, but I couldn't read any more.

"We can talk about this later." Miss V. took the paper. "I'll be back soon."

The door slammed shut behind her.

I tried to turn that article over in my head one little

139

bit at a time, the way I'd seen a pond bird choke down a snake.

A long history of mental issues and instability. Those neighbors were making Mama out to be crazy.

Mama had her mood swings. Every now and then she'd get a bad case of the nerves.

Me and Daddy knew that. It was our family business. *Ours.*

She wasn't crazy. She just needed to stay on her medicine. She wasn't unstable, like some chemical about to explode.

Who did those neighbors think they were?

What did those neighbors know about a mama who smelled of Dove soap and jasmine water and covered my ceiling with midnight-blue-painted eggshell crates and tinfoil stars so I could make a wish every single night?

I knew my mama wasn't like other mamas. In a lot of ways, she was better. As for the rest, it wasn't anything we couldn't deal with.

Still, that line from the article rattled around my head— *long history of mental issues and instability.*

Were all those things I loved about Mama just signs of some craziness I should have had the good sense to spot? Mama would wake me up to have a midnight picnic in the yard. So what if sometimes she'd pin a blanket over the window to keep out the sun, take to bed, and draw her legs up tight against her chest?

When Mama sang along with Hank Williams in the grocery store, the way she'd sing would make me want to howl right along with her. And it wasn't just Hank Williams. There was opera, too—*Madame Butterfly, The Nightingale,* and *Tosca,* and anything else on *World of Opera.* Mama would catch my hand and pull me around the room, making me feel the music.

There was the time Mama took me out of Sunday school to take pictures of a double rainbow. The time Mama drove me around all night long with the sunroof open because I couldn't sleep. The time Mama spent a whole week making me a secret hideout using bamboo, twine, and two types of vines—morning glories, so I'd have flowers in the morning, and moonflowers, to bloom at night.

Mama was just different, that's all.

But what about all the sharp looks in the grocery store? The looks at Mama. The looks at *me.*

If my mama was crazy, just what exactly did that make me?

The floorboards felt like they were shifting. Nothing felt solid. I grabbed hold of the wall.

Is this what going crazy feels like?

Was craziness flowing through my veins, steady as that copperhead's poison?

CHAPTER 32

BEHOLD YOUR WORLD

Out on Miss V.'s back porch, I snatched up her hatchet and hacked at those pine pieces. Whatever those neighbors thought, it didn't bother me one little bit. I was going to find the treasure, and I was going to help Miss V. fix that roof to save Mama's room. I'd do it all.

"You sure you're up to that?" Miss V. looked at me funny.

I got mad all over again, just thinking of those looks in the grocery store.

"I'm fine." I split that pine into splintery bits.

Percy came over and sat, his head turning back and forth. He could have been watching a tennis match, following every little whack of my hatchet, his eyes on that flying wood. One went near him, and he snapped it out of the air, crunched it up, spit it out, and waited for more. I think Percy was just having fun, but it made me feel better to think of him being mad at that wood the way I was mad at those neighbors.

Miss V. fetched herself another hatchet and settled in beside me, a scratched-up book next to her. Soon as Percy saw that book, he sat right down and tilted his ears forward. "By your second-favorite poet," Miss V. announced. "Walt Whitman. We'll pick up where we left off last time." She commenced to reading.

"Do I contradict myself?
Very well then I contradict myself,
(I am large, I contain multitudes.)"

I tried to tune it all out, to just whack away, to let my chopping sound drown out everything else.

When the sun was bright overhead, Miss V. called me to the kitchen and fixed scrambled eggs and bacon for lunch. While the bacon was frying, she went upstairs to check the leak.

We ate with our chairs facing the window. That warm egg smell made the kitchen so full, it took the place of conversation.

I thought Miss V. was thinking about the roof. Instead, she scraped her plate clean, pushed back her chair, and held up a thin blue ribbon.

The ribbon from outside the Bird Room.

It dangled, accusing me.

Miss V. had taken me in. She'd healed me. And I'd gone and done the one thing she told me not to. I'd snooped.

My chin started to quiver.

"I'm sorry. I . . ."

"We had a deal." Miss V. looked more sad than mad.

So I told her. I told her about Mama leaving and Daddy dying and me taking to the woods and how Mama had seen the Bird Room, how she'd met Mr. Bob, about the doogaloo, about the other clues, how people started calling Mama crazy, and how all Mama wanted to do was find the Bird Room, to prove it was real, to see that room one more time. How Mama was coming back day after tomorrow. How the Bird Room could get her to stay. But I didn't tell Miss V. about the last thing I'd said to Mama. Nobody needed to know that.

Miss V. didn't say one single, solitary word until I was done. She waited three full breaths before she opened her mouth.

Inside I felt . . . empty. Like a busted balloon. But also somehow . . . better.

I'd never told a soul anything bad about my mama.

What would Miss V. think of me now that she knew about Mama, now that she knew I hadn't stopped her from leaving?

"Bob wasn't crazy." Miss V. stood up from the table.

"I know he wasn't crazy. I said people were calling my *mama* crazy. That's why I need to show Mama the Bird Room."

"Ace." Her voice got soft. "I've heard about your mama. Maybe your mama's not ready to see you yet. Maybe the room won't change things. Maybe that room isn't good for either one of us. Maybe it's time to go back home to your aunt."

"It's my only chance!" My voice spiraled high. "Please."

I had to think of something to get her to change her mind.

Behind me, Charlene started up her chirping.

My brain churned on empty.

"Be quiet, Charlene," I hard-whispered.

Something else echoed in my head. *Behold.*

Behold your world.

The treasure!

CHAPTER 33

THE ANSWER
TO EVERYTHING

Mama's treasure was the answer to everything.

"What if I could get you some money?" I asked Miss V. "Enough to fix your roof and have some left over." I told her about the treasure note.

"I don't believe it," she said. "The roof needs replacing. You know that. But that room is private. I've never shown it to anybody." She stood up. "There probably isn't any treasure, and who knows if . . ." A pained look flashed, gone as fast as it came. "I tell you what, Ace. I'll give you until day after tomorrow. If you can come up with a treasure by then, we'll split it, and you can show your mother the room."

146

"Thank you, ma'am," I said. "Can we go look at the room? Maybe we could find another clue."

She shook her head. "I don't want you getting your hopes up about any of this. I'm telling you, there isn't any treasure. I clean this house top to bottom every Saturday. Bob left that room over thirty years ago. If there were even a *hint* of treasure, I would have found it by now. Besides, I'm too busy today to go chasing after something that doesn't exist."

"If I help, can I look at the room afterward if there's time?"

Miss V. looked out the window. "We'll see."

My whole plan was hanging on a thin little spiderweb of hope, and here she was, stretching it near to breaking.

✳ ✳ ✳

Percy bounded around the garden, pouncing at every rustle in the grass and running over every few minutes to wiggle his way between me and Miss V. for a right-sided ear rub from Miss V. and a left-sided ear rub from me. I'd spent the afternoon with Miss V., helping her plant and helping her hoe and asking that same question every few minutes: "Can't we take a tiny peek inside the room?"

Each time, Miss V. just shook her head no. Every little while, though, I'd catch her looking at me with a puzzle on her face. Even Percy started cocking his head at me.

After forever, Miss V. went inside, motioned for me to follow, and headed toward the staircase. "Let's take a look at this room you think is going to change things."

She took the key out of her pocket, turned it in the lock, and pushed in the door.

The room sparkled in the sunlight.

Miss V. hiked up her skirt, folded herself cross-legged, and patted the floor beside her.

A silence settled over us.

It felt like sitting in church right after service was over, with holiness still spiking through the air.

I tried to take it all in, to see Mama's room the way she'd seen it.

On the first wall, a fog rose from Miss V.'s garden. The rows were planted in sugar snap peas, the tendrils reaching up in little curls. The trees behind them glowed a bright-eyed green, precise veins on each leaf. Praying mantises dotted the low branches. Ducks perched on a tree, and tanagers sat on limbs and skimmed through the sky, flicking their wings in the sun. Every feather on their bodies was its own shade of red, and every layer showed in the black wings and tails. Wiggles and swiggles wove out from the tanagers, like there was so much personality inside those birds, they bent the air around them. Spring.

The second wall had three painted-over windows. Two more ducks perched on an oak branch. Squirrels scampered down the trunk. Crows glided overhead. Long rows of corn with beans winding up the stalks. The first row started out with no shadow at all. The shadows stretched longer the farther the rows went. Two cicadas made from brown and gray triangles clutched cornstalks near the right corner. Dots and dashes filled the sky nearby, reminding me of music notes. I could almost hear the cicada rhythm. Summer.

Fall was on the next wall, the wall with a window missing a little piece of paint. Glowing orange and red leaves colored the trees. Geese in V formation glided across the sky. The cornstalks hung limp and empty now, and pumpkin vines curved around the floorboards. A mockingbird stared out at me from a gold-leafed sugar maple tree. Seven branches up from the mockingbird, a tanager spread its inky wings to soak up the sunlight, a bit of green now mixed in with the red on its body.

Finally, winter. Bare-naked branches stretched up the wall to an empty sky. Tiny onion and radish plants pierced the garden dirt. Doves roosted low in a shrub down by the baseboard. The winter tanager huddled on a wide oak branch, tucking its wings in tight.

The ceiling was one giant sunflower, shining over us all.

I sat there and watched the light, the ordinary Pickens County sunlight I'd tried to keep from burning my eyes every single day of my life. It shined brightest from the one spot in the fall window without paint. A beam of light crawled across the wall and showed me something new everyplace it landed.

Miss V.'s breath and mine were pulling in at the same time now, going slower the longer we sat there.

The setting sun shimmered on the shiny backs of a little family of ducks. We both let out a soft *ooh*.

Then I saw her. Miss V. was crying, quiet raindrop tears that slid into her cheek folds.

"What happened to Mr. Bob?" I asked.

She just swiped at her face and shook her head. Finally, she stood, her eyes still on those walls. "I knew I shouldn't have come back in this room. Better not stay in here too long, Ace. Paint fumes might get to us."

But any fool could tell you that paint had been dry for years. All I could smell was Miss V., the rust scent from something she'd been holding, and the rosemary water she must have used on her face.

I stayed put.

"Miss V., Mr. Bob said to follow the light. He said to start with the treasure in your house." I pulled the note out of the knothole and showed her.

"Well, I'll be. . . ." Miss V. studied the wall. "But I still don't think Bob had a treasure. I'm the one who took him in after he walked out of the woods, empty-pocketed and with a bad case of the nerves. He didn't even trust me at first, and we grew up friends. It was all I could do to get him halfway calm. The only things that worked were getting him to help me with my puzzles and just leaving him alone. Letting him tromp around the woods, carving and painting and doing whatever else he wanted to do."

I pointed at the words. "He said to start with the treasure in this house."

Miss V. put the note back in the hole and gave it a little pat. "It's all foolishness. That's not the way Bob talked at all. He didn't use words like 'treasure.'"

Treasure. Treasure. I'd come across that word somewhere else in her house.

The answer had to be on Miss V.'s doily-covered bookcase.

CHAPTER 34

DEAD END

Miss V.'s copy of *Treasure Island* had seen better days. Faded circle watermarks on the cover, smudges and stains speckling the page edges. The binding was cracked, too.

Still, there was that word, right in the title. "Miss V., this has to be the treasure in your house that Mr. Bob meant in his note."

She looked like she didn't believe me.

A splinter of an idea pricked at my brain. "You said doing your puzzles helped calm Mr. Bob down."

She gave a slow nod.

"Maybe there's a puzzle in this book. A secret code. Like when somebody underlines letters or words."

Miss V. hunted down a pencil and paper.

I flipped through the book. Nothing but print all the way to page 72. Then, on page 72, *TURN TO P. 218.*

Miss V. shook her head. "It wouldn't be that easy. Keep going."

Page 218: *TURN TO P. 86.*

Okay. Page 86: *TURN TO P. 146.*

I did. *TURN TO P. 260.*

Page 260: *Steps outside* was underlined.

Miss V. shook her head. "It's a dead end, Ace."

A dead end. If the treasure was hidden outside, how would we *ever* find it?

From her cage, Charlene chirped. Three long blasts. *Yant, yant, YANT.* From where I was standing, it sounded an awful lot like "Don't give up."

Miss V. stood. She was giving up.

I slammed the book on the couch.

The front cover slid to one side, and the pages fanned.

Spread out, the smudges and smears on the sides of the pages lined up in a crooked kind of way.

I eased the front cover over, just a smidgen.

A shape. I adjusted the pages. It was a tiny tanager in flight. To the side of it, letters—*CONSTELLATION AT 5:30 IN MY ROOM AT THE MAGIC HOUR.*

Another tanager! We had to be close.

Then I realized—there wasn't a constellation in the

153

Bird Room. There was nothing on that ceiling except a giant sunflower.

We were at another dead end.

So why was Miss V. standing over my shoulder and grinning for all get-out?

CHAPTER 35

CONSTELLATION

We've missed the magic hour today, Ace. We can try tomorrow." Miss V. squeezed the book back onto the shelf.

"What's the magic hour?"

Miss V. pointed out the window. "It's the hour just before the sun goes down, when everything glows golden. Bob's favorite time. He loved to see what the light did to his paintings. Five-thirty at the magic hour is five-thirty p.m. He wanted us to see where the sun shines in his room then."

I thought about the way that the paint on the fall window focused the light into a beam. It reminded me of the way I'd used sunlight to start my fire. *"Follow the light."* I nodded. "So, what do we do now?"

"We do what needs doing. If there really *is* a treasure, we can't do anything about finding it until tomorrow evening. And you need to find us a constellation." She went to the kitchen and started pulling out pots to make dinner.

I trailed along behind her, chopping onions and celery like she told me to and finally breathing in the rich smell of her gumbo. But something bothered me. If the magic hour was the hour *before* the sun went down, how were we supposed to find a constellation?

Soon as dinner was over, I sat out on the porch, trying to ignore Percy howling like a coyote, and watched the moonlight shadows shift into one another. I searched the sky for constellations. Mama used to tell me that when she was little, the moon followed her. On my eighth birthday, Mama gave me her moon. She said it could be my pet, too. "Even if I'm not here," Mama said, "you know my moon is watching over you."

All of a sudden, I felt extra cold. When Mama said she'd give me the moon to watch over me, was she thinking about leaving, even back then? Was she like that mama bird, getting ready to fly off and leave me and the nest behind?

A thought popped into my head, and I couldn't push it away: Aunt Belinda didn't fly off. She woke up at the same time every day, got dressed first thing every morning, kept her kitchen clean, and put supper on the table every night.

She bought me graph paper for school even when she couldn't scrape together enough cash to get those dark roots of hers dyed blond again.

After Uncle Quinn up and ran off with a neighbor woman, Aunt Belinda didn't fall to pieces the way most folks reckoned she would. Not even after word got out about how he'd greased her finger while she was asleep and slipped off her wedding ring to sell, cash for gold. She just wrote thank-you notes for the casseroles, took to wearing boxing gloves to bed, slathered a smile on her lips every morning, and started selling Wanda's Classy Lady beauty products on the side when her receptionist job didn't pay all the bills. She covered up that *Hot Stuff* tattoo my uncle had talked her into, back before they had kids. She made those boys of hers tuck in their shirttails, and she marched them off to church every Sunday like she didn't have a thing in the world to be ashamed of.

It was only at night, when I guess she thought nobody could hear her, that I heard the cry sounds coming from her room.

Which got me to wondering. Would I be better off with someone who toughed it out and stayed around—even if she was miserable—or was I better off with a mama who'd up and leave whenever she got the notion but would drive me all the way to Jackson just to show me paintings, a mama who liked my drawing best of all?

A cardinal *chit-chit*ted from somewhere I couldn't see. Why couldn't Mama be like a cardinal and stick around all year?

Sitting out there on that cold wood porch, I wanted my mama back so bad, I didn't care whether she wanted to be back or not.

CHAPTER 36

DIRT

One day till Mama. One day till Mama. I chanted it in my head. We had one night left to find a constellation, and what did Miss V. care about?

Shoveling chicken poop, that's what.

Soon as breakfast was over, she motioned for me to follow her out to the garden. "Can't find a constellation until tonight."

"But shouldn't we be looking . . ."

Miss V. just shook her head. "Have to keep the dirt healthy." She went to work on something else.

I spent the morning shoveling stuff I didn't want to touch or smell into the garden rows, Charlene keeping me company. Percy, he was having a big time rolling around in it all. He was as excited about that stirred-up chicken poop as Mama and I had been the last time it snowed. He flopped on his back, spread out his back legs, and wiggled around, making little chicken-poop angels.

Dirt is funny stuff. Daddy used to say that if you stick to suburbs and sidewalks your whole life, dirt all looks the same. But when good dirt means the difference between eating and going hungry, it starts to look right particular. Daddy told me about how after they moved out of this town into the country, his *own* daddy put him in charge of the dirt for their garden.

Daddy taught me how to turn coffee grounds and dried-up leaves into the kind of dark, crumbly dirt that could convince a vegetable garden to keep putting out produce through a dry spell. Come spring, Daddy would sift the dirt pile, add sand or ashes, and work it into the garden. He wouldn't let me plant the first seed until the dirt had the right feel. Especially not Mama's row of sunflowers. We had to plant that row last, and it had to be plumb perfect and raked smooth.

I knew not even dying could keep Daddy from taking note of the dirt.

Daddy always said that when his time came, he wanted to be buried near his kinfolks in the Big Ridge cemetery, not near a ghost town. But I don't think he knew what was lying under all that Bermuda grass in that graveyard. I saw the clay the day before his funeral, when I was supposed to be standing next to Aunt Belinda in the receiving line inside the Fellowship Hall and letting everybody hug my neck.

Instead, I'd slunk out to the graveyard behind the church and kicked over every anthill I could find. *How could Mama not even show up for her own husband's visitation?*

Then my eyes lit on that puke-colored clay.

The next day, the day of Daddy's funeral, they'd found Mama. She walked in late, but I ran to her soon as I saw her. She didn't look herself, stiff and pale in a new black dress, like the starch was holding her up. We'd have time to talk later, I thought. She could explain everything. We just had to get through the service first.

When it was time to put Daddy's coffin in the ground, I couldn't stand the thought of Daddy in that slick, ugly clay. When the preacher called me up to throw a shovelful of dirt on his coffin, I bent down, unbuckled the black patent-leather purse Grandma had given me three Easters back, and filled my shovel with the best dirt from Mama's flower row. The dirt was black and coarse as brownie crumbs, and I sprinkled it all up and down the head end of the coffin.

I don't think one single soul saw what I did. Everybody

else was too busy watching Mama, wondering *right out loud, where I could hear it,* where they'd found her. Aunt Belinda whispered to the preacher's wife how they'd had to search high and low to find Mama and bring her back for the funeral, how they'd had to give her something to keep her calm, and how they were going to sit her down afterward and try to get her to act right and stay for good. For the record, Aunt Belinda isn't any good at whispering.

Back in the chairs, Mama stretched out one scratchy long sleeve toward me, but she kept her body angled away.

I couldn't stop shaking, not even when Aunt Belinda squeezed in next to me and jangled her bangle-covered arm all up and down my back.

Mama didn't so much as look at me from the time the preacher told us all to sit down till the last song was over. She just clutched her closed hand against her stomach. And she didn't say goodbye, either. One minute, she was standing there next to me, and the next she was missing again.

Like I'd imagined her in the first place.

Daddy was dead, and all I'd gotten from Mama was a nod and a squint from eyes that looked as empty as a winter sky.

But tomorrow would be different, wouldn't it?

Back inside Miss V.'s kitchen, I washed up in the sink and flipped open the cabinet, looking for a glass.

Stuck to the inside of the cabinet door with crackled tape was the question Miss V. had asked me.

MONDAY'S QUESTION:

ONLY ONE COLOR BUT NOT ONE SIZE.

STUCK AT THE BOTTOM, YET EASILY FLIES.

ANSWER ON FRIDAY.

BOB

If Miss V. had asked me that question, I guess she never did get her answer.

I eased the cabinet door back closed.

Me and Miss V., we were both wandering around, wondering things.

I didn't have an answer for Miss V., and I sure didn't have an answer for me.

163

CHAPTER 37

THE STOKES SCHOOL

It must have been along about lunchtime when Miss V. walked into the kitchen and handed me the latest issue of the *Messenger*. Percy had chewed the whole bottom part off, but I could still read the top.

HOPE WANES FOR MISSING GIRL

Continuing searches have turned up no sign of Ariana "Cricket" Overland.

Mrs. Bullard, art teacher at East Pickens Middle School, reported that the loss was particularly tragic because a sketch done by Cricket had just won the Fluhrer

164

Prize at the prestigious Stokes School for the Arts in Jackson, winning her a place in the weeklong spring-break camp for middle school students, beginning March 3. Past winners of the Fluhrer Prize have gone on to gain admission to the Stokes high school program. Mrs. Bullard reported that "Cricket's work showed such promise. We are all mourning the tragic events that have surrounded her."

Meanwhile, the victim's aunt, Belinda Overland, has kept up her vigil at the fire station, providing free samples of Classy Lady lip balm to the firemen. "Even at a time like this," she said, "it's important to keep moisturized."

"Congratulations," Miss V. said. "So you're an artist, too. But people are really missing you, Ace. Maybe it's time to head back."

"Tomorrow," I said. "A deal's a deal."

She sighed and went off for more chores.

I knew just exactly which drawing of mine Mrs. Bullard must have sent in—that drawing of Mama standing in front of a mirror with her hands folded under her chin.

After Mama left, I was scared I'd forget what she looked like. I mean, what she *really* looked like, not just when she put on her camera smile for pictures.

I couldn't stop working on that drawing. When I was sketching, I forgot where I was. I could pretend Mama was sitting right there next to me, sketching too. It took me a week of study halls and a mess of grubby eraser bits to get my picture halfway decent-looking.

I was going to tape it on the inside of my notebook, where I could see it whenever I wanted.

But it was funny. As soon as I laid down the last pencil stroke, I couldn't bring myself to look at it. My picture had no more life in it than a shadow on a dark-gray wall.

All my picture did was remind me—Mama had left me.

When Mrs. Bullard asked if she could have it, I was glad to see that picture go.

Now my drawing was the reason the Stokes School wanted to have me at their spring-break camp.

It just figured. The one good thing that had happened since Mama took off, and I'd be too busy getting Mama settled to go to the camp. And that was if everything went my way.

But, sure as shooting, I was fixing to make certain that everything did.

CHAPTER 38

THE MAGIC HOUR

"It's the magic hour." Miss V. turned her key in the lock.

I followed, Charlene on my shoulder.

The magic was already showing itself.

The walls glowed with slanty sunlight through the painted-over windows.

The light was soft except for that one bare place on the fall window. There, the light became a bright yellow spotlight. It lit across the pea tendrils, just like the ones in Miss V.'s garden.

I spread my hand on the springtime wall. It felt like the garden was growing even as we watched. This room was full of paintings of the things from Miss V.'s garden.

Mr. Bob's clue had to mean to look where the light landed at exactly five-thirty. Soon, the light would land on some plant or tree from Miss V.'s garden, and that would tell us where to dig.

Outside, the sun sank lower in the sky. It took five minutes for the spotlight to ease off the garden rows. My watch told us when it was five-thirty. By then, the light had moved across my hand and come to rest on a praying mantis on a dogwood branch.

The light lingered on the bug and then slowly slid up the wall as the last of the daylight faded and disappeared outside.

No constellation.

"That can't be right," Miss V. said. "I've got bugs all over my garden. That isn't the puzzle piece."

Charlene crawled around my shoulder to drive home the point.

Miss V. and Charlene were right. A praying mantis didn't have a thing in the world to do with a constellation. The light hadn't shown us where to dig.

Two more paint chips fluttered off the ceiling and landed at my feet.

No constellation. No treasure.

Miss V. put her shoulder to the door. "Sorry, Ace. We tried."

CHAPTER 39

VALENTINE'S CHOCOLATES

I sat on the front porch and stewed, Charlene sitting on my shoulder.

Percy came over, laid his big head in my lap, looked up at me with sad eyes, and started licking up a storm on my hand. He could tell how I felt. Charlene did, too. She stroked her antennae against my neck and let out a *yant* that echoed like a sigh.

Above me, the sky was bright with a thousand constellations that couldn't help me one bit. The only things out with us were a bunch of moths. They flung themselves against the front windows, leaving little chalky marks.

Stupid moths.

Mama was already on her way. She'd be here tomorrow, and I wouldn't have her treasure.

And what would happen to Miss V.? The nights were cold, with the dark still coming so early. With her house falling apart, how long could she make it out here?

Wait a minute.

A good thought had just flickered across my mind. It was like the taste that lingers in your mouth after a piece of Valentine's chocolate.

I tried to catch hold. Charlene crouched down on my shoulder. She was thinking, too.

Percy wagged his black tail at me, and Charlene took a little jump. She landed on my arm and looked at me with her deep, dark eyes.

That's it!

With the dark still coming so early.

Of course the dark was still coming so early. It was February.

With spring on the way, the sun set a little later every day.

Mr. Bob wrote his note on March 6, the same day as Mama's birthday. The light would be different that day. But how?

CHAPTER 40

SUNSETS

"We need to talk about daylight."

Miss V. looked up from the poetry books she was pluck-ing off the shelf. She drew her brows together. "You tak-ing up farming?" She went to the door and held out some books.

Percy scratched the Dickinson near to pieces. She sat down and started up reading.

"A winged spark doth soar about—
I never met it near
For Lightning it is oft mistook
When nights are hot and sere—"

I paced the porch while she finished. "That poem even drives home my point."

Miss V. shut the book. "Make some sense, will you?"

"That poem talked about when days are hot and sere. That means summer, right? The days are longer in summer."

"Go on."

"And spring is coming. The days are getting longer."

"Of course." She looked like she had better things to do.

"Today is February twenty-eighth, right?"

"Right." Her voice was wary.

"Mr. Bob's note was written on March sixth, not February twenty-eighth. The sun would have set at a different time. If we could just figure out how to tell how much different it would be, we could solve that clue."

Miss V.'s eyes lit up. She marched to the bookcase, sorted through the spines of the books for about five minutes, and came back with a copy of the 1984 edition of the *Mississippi Gardener's Almanac*. "We have all we need right here."

Ha! That book would have sunset times!

She handed it to me. I flipped it open and looked for the Deerfield section. I found February. Then I traced my finger to February 26 . . . *Sunset: 5:48;* February 27 . . . *Sunset: 5:49.*

Then I came to February 28:

Sunset: 5:50

I flipped to the date of the letter, March 6:

Sunset: 5:55

I showed her. "So on the day Mr. Bob wrote that note, the sunset would have been five minutes later. Sunlight from the window would have shined on a different spot. It took five minutes for the spot to move across my hand. What we're looking for has to be one hand size away."

"Poetry saves the day," Miss V. said, and headed for the stairs.

Back in the room, I shifted over a bit and measured one hand width up the wall from the praying mantis. It landed on a tanager.

But that room had lots of tanagers. What was special about this one?

Miss V. held up the lantern, and we both studied that bird.

"Look at its mouth." I pointed.

That tanager held a tiny star in its beak. The same kind of star as the one carved in the woods. The same kind of star as the one carved on that contraption in Miss V.'s piano.

But where does that get us?

Then I measured with my hand again. That sunlight spot wouldn't shine on the whole tanager. It would shine on the star. "One star. Okay. So far, so good. Now we have to figure out how to turn that one star into a whole constellation."

Now Miss V. was the one doing the pointing. A faint dotted line started at that star and made its way down the wall, weaving in and out of branches and weeds.

Miss V. traced the star line with her finger. "Twenty dashed lines, Ace."

Most of the other dots and lines on the mural seemed to be random—some short, some long. These twenty lines were all the same distance. They ended in a tiny X.

"Like footsteps on a treasure map. X marks the spot," I said. I remembered those underlined words from *Treasure Island: Steps outside.*

Except that the X was over a tangle of vines that didn't seem to match up with Miss V.'s garden at all.

Miss V. said what I was thinking. "But if they *are* footsteps, we've still got to figure out how to match this up with a real place. We've got to find a constellation to know where to start walking."

A constellation. All I knew about constellations was from science class—"a configuration of stars." I ran my hand back over the star on the wall.

The writing below the star was so little, it looked like fine brushstrokes. But there it was:

WORTHY #1

That's when it hit me. I knew where to start.
I should have known it the whole time.

STAR TO STAR

Percy pranced ahead of us, sniffing the air, digging a hole every ten feet or so and circling back to nudge at me with his muddy nose. I patted him and wiped the mud off my hands. "Almost there."

When that lantern light hit the tanager tree, Miss V. and Percy both jumped back. Percy growled.

Then Miss V. eased up on that tanager and ran her fingers over the star. "Well, I'll be. . . . Worthy #3."

"Now here's where the puzzle part comes in." I handed her the contraption I'd taken from her piano. Worthy #2. "Star to star. A constellation."

She smiled. "Do you even know what this is?"

I shook my head no.

"It's a dowser. It vibrates when there's something underground. My daddy used it to find the right place to dig a well. Bob carved on it and turned it into his own creation."

She held out the two shovels she'd brought. "How many dashes before the X?"

"Twenty."

Miss V. pointed. "In the painting, it was south. That-a-ways."

She touched the star on the dowsing rod to the star on the tanager tree, held the dowser out in front, and measured off twenty even steps from the south side of the tree.

Nothing.

"You try it, Ace." She handed me the dowser. "Maybe you've got the touch. Hold it loose. Let the rods guide you."

Twenty marks on the mural.

I tried to think of how a man would walk it.

Big steps.

I stretched mine out for twenty long paces.

Something was happening.

The contraption quivered in my hands.

Miss V. had seen it, too. "Trust the dowser."

Tightening my grip, I followed it deeper into the woods.

The quivering didn't change until I breathed in the sweet smell of the tea olive trees growing at the edge of the Pickens County Baptist Cemetery.

Miss V. turned up the flame on the lantern. "That son of a gun," she said.

CHAPTER 42

GRAVE ROBBING

Just say the words "grave robbing," and it brings to mind something a heap sight more exciting than what me, Percy, and Miss V. were doing. Come to find out, grave robbing is mostly just digging.

It was all heave, take a shovel load, dump it out, beat the shovel against the side of the hole to shake off the clay, and start over again. And the whole time, Miss V. was digging faster than me.

It's downright embarrassing to get outworked by somebody six times your age.

I guess you can't always tell strong from the outside.

Percy, he was running back and forth between us,

digging every time he stopped, throwing out a huge clay trail behind him.

The dowser had led us to a sandstone rock laid flat in the dirt in the corner of the cemetery, near the first tanager rock I'd found.

"It's all making sense now," Miss V. said. "This is my family's cemetery plot. Those are my mama's initials. Of course Bob would end the clue trail here."

We dug faster.

The wind whistled through the gravestones. A screech owl let out a shuddery cry.

The whole place spooked up my arm hairs.

Grandma, I hope you're looking out for me.

Miss V. started humming—"Nearer, My God, to Thee."

In a weird way, I'd miss her after I left with Mama tomorrow. There was something about Miss V. I couldn't quite put my finger on. But she knew who she was. She was storm steady, like my ginkgo tree. And she'd trusted me through all these clue trails she didn't believe in.

After a while, the hole opened up around us like it had been waiting for us all those years.

What Miss V. was thinking about, I had no idea, and she kept that to herself. Me, all I could think about was seeing Mama.

I worked out in my head how it would go. I wouldn't

want to just jump out of the woods at her. If I showed up too sudden, I might scare her away.

I'd leave her a sign so I could ease her into thinking about me. Then I'd come up slow so she could see me coming. I'd spread out my arms and hug her tight. With nobody else around, I could talk to Mama good. I could tell her I was sorry. I could tell her about the Bird Room. She wasn't crazy. She hadn't imagined it. I'd tell her all that. I'd get her to stay.

A *thud* echoed.

Had Miss V. run her shovel into a root?

She dug her shovel in that spot a second time.

A metal-hitting-metal sound rang out.

We'd found it!

We carved the dirt out from the edges and heaved it out of the hole.

It was a metal case about the size of a suitcase.

We had the treasure! I went over to Grandma's wooden headstone and drew a cricket in the dirt. I drew it big and bold where Mama would see it right off.

Tomorrow, everything that mattered would be right again, most of all Mama and me.

CHAPTER 43

A THOUSAND MILES

"Let's see what Bob left us." Miss V. patted the case on her kitchen table.

I unsnapped the buckles and opened it.

But all I saw were sticks of chalk and a bundle of cloth gone gray and spotty.

I held my breath, waiting for the sparkle of gold. Or rubies. Or diamonds. Or *something*. But the bundle smelled like dirt and rain and old sweaters as Miss V. unwound it.

It was just a pile of typing paper, wrinkled and crinkled by the cloth.

My stomach drew itself into a lopsided knot.

I almost got myself killed over a stack of paper.

182

The note. The stars. The constellation.

Mama.

After all those clues, how could there not be treasure?

Disappointment squirrel-jumped through every single part of me.

But beside me, Miss V. let out a whoop. "I should have known. . . ." She started spreading out the sheets.

A glimmer of red caught my eye—a tanager, flying high over Miss V.'s woods. It was aiming for the last ray of light shining on the tallest limb of a black walnut tree.

"The golden hour." Miss V. grinned.

I leaned into the sheets.

That paper held drawings and watercolor paintings of Miss V.'s woods. Of my woods. The woods I'd tramped through, the greens I'd eaten, the squirrels nesting above me, the raccoons who'd stole my food. Even a rough-sketched coyote.

Someone had made all those things with a quick-lined *rightness.* Every detail that mattered stood out—the eyes, the fur, the fold of a leg, the shadow of a fern leaf. Spirals echoed out from the figures in an exclamation-mark kind of way.

When I was out in those woods, the plants and animals seemed to me like separate things to eat or stay away from. I thought they were no more a part of each other than I was a part of them. But on those pages, those woods and plants and animals fit together in a rhythm.

"Well, it isn't cash money, but I can't say I'm mad about it." Miss V. ran her fingers along the edge of a painting of five green-headed ducks.

She leaned back and I studied those papers. Some pictures weren't much more than thin pencil strokes. But they showed more than I could ever say in a lifetime about a raccoon or a dragonfly or a duck. I'd never seen anybody make fine art out of just plain old woods things.

I'd never thought that doing a painting of something you saw every day of your life could change the way you looked at it.

I brought out Charlene to see it all.

To Miss V.'s credit, she didn't say one word about a cricket crawling all over those pictures.

"Would you mind telling me about Mr. Bob? Why would he hide this?"

Miss V. got us each some water from the sink and sat back down, careful to keep the glasses away from the pictures.

"Bob was my best friend growing up. Until I was ten, my family lived on the coast, near his. We used to explore the woods together. He wanted to be a professional artist. He loved drawing and painting as much as I loved puzzles and riddles. Even after my family moved up here to take over Papa's homeplace and keep the timber farm going, Bob still came to visit from time to time. Then, for no reason I could figure, he just stopped coming. Stopped writing, too.

"After I got my degree, I took a job in Jackson, teaching literature at a junior college. Then Mama and Papa got sick, and I came back here to take care of them. I kept writing Bob, even though he never wrote back. Then one day, years later, not long after Mama and Papa died, I was out working in the garden like I knew what I was doing. I was trying to get up the gumption to carry on what they'd started, wondering if I should give up."

Miss V. took a sip and held it in her mouth before she swallowed.

I had a sudden urge to wrap my arms around her. But Miss V. was drawn up too stiff in her seat.

"So right out of the blue, Bob shows up, worn out and missing a shoe."

She touched a drawing of a luna moth. "Bob asked if he could rest here for a few days. Course I said yes. Told him he could stay as long as he wanted." Miss V. eased back in her chair. "I put him in the upstairs bedroom. Every day, he'd set out with nothing but his carving knife, paper, and watercolors. And every day, he'd bring me back a piece of the woods, drawn on that paper. At night, he'd help me work on my puzzles and riddles. He started to love them almost as much as I did."

Miss V. shifted in her seat. "Come to find out, he'd just

left a mental hospital. Before that, his art had started to get noticed, and he'd been asked to paint a mural in a library. But his art was different, and a lot of people didn't understand it."

She looked at the wall behind me. "Sometimes different makes people uncomfortable."

I thought of all those looks at Mama in the grocery store.

For the first time since I'd met her, Miss V.'s shoulders drooped. "They made Bob change his design. Another mural got canceled. Later, there was even a call to paint over some of his work." She cut her eyes to the dark window. "Bob took it hard."

Some walls aren't for everyone. Maybe Mr. Bob didn't just mean the winter tanager. Maybe he meant his own murals. Maybe he meant himself, too.

Everything else started sliding into place. *Behold your world. Seek the beauty.* Maybe sometimes you need to go through the uncomfortable to find your way to the beautiful. It takes some adjusting in the way you look at things to really see them. Sometimes you need to squint and sometimes you need to open your eyes wider and sometimes you need to look at things from the other side.

"Maybe that's why Mr. Bob made it so hard," I said. "For someone to find his paintings, they'd have to study the room. They'd have to work through all his clues."

"I think you're right, Ace." Miss V. grinned. "And you solved it."

"What happened to Mr. Bob?"

"He's gone now. He died too young. But he *did* become a famous artist. When he showed up here, though, he was just my old friend, still drawing, still painting. He was on his way back home to his family. He walked the whole way. A thousand miles."

I pictured all that walking Mama did, looking for the Bird Room. I pictured all those scarlet tanagers, migrating over a thousand miles. "Why do you think he decided to pay you a visit?" I asked.

Miss V. leaned forward in her chair. "Bob had a bad case of the nerves by the time he got here. He was scratched up and bruised. He needed to heal up."

She traced her fingers across a drawing of morning glory vines. "I thought I could help him find more peace, but I couldn't." She rubbed at her neck. "I didn't see the room until after Bob left. My great-great-great-grandfather built that room during the Civil War to hide his sons so they wouldn't have to go fight. We always kept it closed off.

"Bob painted that whole room in the time it took me to plant my spring garden. When he left, he put the key to that room behind the picture, and he left me a doogaloo, painted the same way that you said yours was. I thought he took his paintings with him."

Miss V. stretched back in her chair. "Bob could have marched right out the front door in the daylight with my blessing." The edges of her mouth turned up. "But that wasn't Bob's way. No sirree. A week before he left, he made me promise not to touch that room. Said it was private. That looking at it would be the same as reading his diary. Then one night, Bob knotted four of my sheets together and slid out the second-floor window without even saying goodbye. He took a bar of soap and drew a flock of tanagers on the side of my house the whole way down. Wouldn't you know it, each little bird was pointed south, just like where Bob was headed."

I closed my eyes, and I could just see that flock of birds floating down the side of the house.

Miss V. tightened her jaw. "A few years later, the whole town up and cleared out. Left behind nothing but stumps and sidewalks. But I'd come to love this land. My family'd been here since before that town came. I wanted to stay here after."

Miss V. turned the glass in her hand. "Every so often, I'd get a painting or a letter in the mail. No return address, but I was glad to see Bob kept painting. In his letters, he said he liked to row his boat out to a little island. He'd stay out there by himself and paint for days. Said folks were calling him crazy for taking off like that."

She leaned back. "People said things about your friend Emily Dickinson, too." Miss V. looked toward the living room shelves. "They said she was different, that she kept to herself. Some people even claimed she wore white all the time. But things people said can't make her poems any less beautiful. You know her poems." She jabbed at a paper with her first finger. "And you look at these paintings. You tell me who's crazy and who's not."

I ran my fingers along the smooth white petals of a gardenia Bob had painted. It was so perfect, I could almost smell it.

Miss V. put her hand next to mine. "Bob just carried on the best he knew how. Maybe like your mother. You know, your daddy was my second cousin once removed. I know about your mother."

I jerked my hand away.

You're wrong. My mama wasn't crawling out of windows, traipsing all over the country with a missing shoe.

Miss V. patted my arm. "I'm not saying your mother is just like Bob. What I'm saying is, she probably did the best she could, the same way he did. Whatever those neighbors said about her, that isn't who she is. Remember the line from that Walt Whitman poem, 'I am large, I contain multitudes'?" Your mama's more than what those neighbors think, and you know it. She's a person like anyone else. She has her struggles and her strengths. Your mama loves you. Leaving you must have been the hardest thing she ever did. She must have had a mighty good reason to do it."

I pressed my fingers down into the painting, trying to feel how Mr. Bob must have felt when he made that flower. Anything but listen to Miss V. She didn't know Mama. She didn't know me.

Miss V.'s voice got soft. "You can go ahead and show your mama that room." She covered my hand.

The heat of her hand melted into mine, natural as two spoons nesting together in a drawer. Her fingers were Percy-warm.

She smoothed out a wrinkle in a picture with her other hand. "You don't have to go, you know. You can stay here with me. Seeing how we're family and all. I mean, if things don't work out with your mother. Your mother might not be ready for things to work out. Not just yet."

I'd near about died for a chance to see Mama, and here Miss V. was, fixing to jinx it. I scraped back from the table and tried to keep the mad out of my voice. "No thank you."

She pulled her mouth into a tight smile and took her glass to the sink. "It's past bedtime. You'd better get some rest before you go meet your mother."

I stretched. All that digging had worked tiredness into every single muscle.

Under the soft blankets on Miss V.'s daybed, I dreamed of gardenias. Big, luscious gardenias, the kind Mr. Bob might have drawn. In my dream, me and Mama gathered a basket full of blossoms and breathed in deep.

The smell faded as soon as my eyes popped open.

Bright sunlight filled the room.

I was late for the one thing I'd been working toward since I set out from Thelma's Cash 'n' Carry.

CHAPTER 44

MAMA DAY

I didn't even have to ask Charlene if she wanted to come meet Mama. She jumped right up and burrowed into the collar of Daddy's jacket. Miss V. had sewn the top button back on, and I buttoned it tight to keep Charlene close. Percy, he just stayed on the porch, tail a-wagging. It was like he knew this was something me and Charlene needed to do by ourselves.

Mama never was an early riser, and I prayed the whole way out to the sidewalk that she wouldn't be one today. I wanted to get there first.

Around me, the woods had changed. The sun lit on new

white blooms everywhere. Even the dewdrops dotting my pant legs were the color of spring.

Mama day was here!

But a part of me felt like it'd come too fast. I got that forgot-to-study-for-a-math-test feeling deep down in my gut.

Climbing the hill to the graveyard, I steered around an overgrown willow. I'd made Mama a walking stick out of willow last summer. After Grandma died, Mama took so many walks and stumbled around so much when she got back that I figured she could use a good walking stick. Daddy showed me how, and I carved her a cane with a sunflower on the handle.

Mama admired that walking stick from every angle and set off on her walk that first day holding it high.

Two weeks later, I found the stick poking out from behind a pizza box by the trash can. It was snapped in two pieces.

I didn't ask. I didn't want to know.

I'd probably picked out a weak branch. You never can tell where the fault line is with some wood.

Still, doubt crept in on little roach feet. Maybe Mama wouldn't show. Maybe I couldn't get her to stay.

Everything felt like one big stack of maybes. It was piled high and teetering, and I just hoped it wasn't about to fall.

As I stepped over the cemetery fence, I shaped my breath into a prayer. *Let her come here. Make her stay. Let her come here. Make her stay.*

Then, just like that, there she was.

Mama was crouching with her back to me, stroking a new pink-marble headstone covered in doves and lambs.

Mama!

I ran two steps forward.

And stopped.

Something was different. Mama's long hair was gone. Her chopped-off hair stopped at her chin. And her head was turned. She was talking to somebody off to the side.

A man stepped out from behind the tree.

He wore a hat the color of a stinkbug, the kind no self-respecting cowboy would be caught dead in. "Excuse me, hon. I had to answer nature's call. Least I got you here, right on schedule." His voice was fake-cheery. He sounded like a radio announcer trying to sell car insurance.

The man held out his hand, probably the one he'd just answered nature's call with, and helped Mama up. He draped his arm around her shoulder.

Around my mama.

My insides lurched.

I sprang out of the woods to push him off Mama.

Mama saw me first. She shook her head like her brain couldn't get ahold of what she was seeing.

Then she broke out in that birthday-cake smile of hers. "Cricket! What are you doing here?" She spread her arms wide. "You get over here and hug my neck!"

Mama stepped away from the man and swooped me right up. My lungs filled with her Dove-soap-and-jasmine smell. I could swim around in that smell forever and never come up for air. It was worth every single thing I'd gone through to get here.

I let out the breath of stale air I'd been holding in since the day Mama left. She was back! Nothing else mattered. Everything was right.

Only it wasn't.

Mama's hug was off-center.

When she let go, Mama leaned back at a slant.

My mama's belly was swole out. It was throwing her off balance.

The man reached forward to help her, his eyes on her stomach the whole time.

And I knew.

Mama was carrying a baby.

A baby that didn't have one single thing to do with Daddy, and didn't have one single thing to do with me.

Mama clutched at my arm and patted her stomach.

"You're going to be a big sister, Cricket. And I'd like you to meet Brian."

The man stepped forward and held out his hand. "It's a pleasure to meet you."

I kept my hands stuck to my sides.

A bright-red cardinal landed on the fence post and *chit-chit*ted. Fast as he got there, he flew off, disappearing behind a thick tangle of briars.

This was the same exact spot where I'd been with Mama last summer. The same exact spot I'd nearly died to get to. The same exact spot where Grandma was supposed to help me set things right.

And now everything was wrong.

Brian dropped his hand. "We, uh, hadn't exactly planned on seeing you this trip." He jammed a hand in his pocket. "But we did want to see you. As soon as we're all settled, we wanted you to come stay with us."

Mama stroked my cheek with the back of her feathery fingers. "I'm living outside Memphis now. Brian and I are getting married. Brian has a great big house with a rose garden and a fishpond and a fountain. He put tanager sculptures all over the backyard, just for me. You'll love it. You'll see."

Mama started talking faster, using the voice she used with company. "I'm going to fix up a room for you, Cricket. Brian will buy you a sky-blue canopy bed and all the clothes

196

you want. Brian keeps things real nice." She patted the top of my head like I was three.

I grabbed hold of her hand. "You don't have to go back to Memphis, Mama. Our home is *here*." Her hand felt too cold, and I rubbed her fingers against my cheek. "I found the Bird Room. You were right, Mama. It's just the way you said. The light on the walls makes the paintings look alive. You weren't crazy, Mama. That room is *real*. I even found the buried surprise—paintings like you've never seen before. I've been staying with a nice lady, kin to Daddy, and that room is in her house. I can take you there right now."

Just for an instant, Mama's face lit up. "The Bird Room."

But then her eyes looked past me, and she shook her head.

"It wasn't a painting, Cricket. That room really *was* alive. I saw that tanager flutter its wings." Mama rubbed at the side of her neck. "I told you that."

Brian stood behind Mama and kneaded her shoulders. "You've been doing so good, honey. Let's not get over-excited. It's almost time for lunch." He shot me a look.

Who is he to tell me how to act around my own mama?

Mama leaned back into his hands. "Now, should we buy slaw dogs or barbecue for lunch? You're going to have to decide for us, Cricket."

I held Mama's hand tight and lowered my voice into a fierce whisper. "That room is less than a mile from where we're standing. I can take you there right this minute." I pulled at her hand.

She stayed put.

I pulled harder. "Come on, Mama! *Grandma* would want you to see it."

Mama didn't budge. Her eyebrows bunched together. She combed at her hair with her fingers.

I leaned my full weight into her arm.

She pulled the other way, and her hand slipped from mine.

She steadied herself. "No, baby, it's time to head back to Memphis. I've got the headstone aligned just right. It's perfect. You'll see. Brian wants to beat the traffic. Come with us. There's a big backseat."

I thought about a cozy canopy bed in a room near Mama. I wanted to crawl up in that bed and feel Mama's soft hands on my back.

Charlene let out a soft *yant, yant,* and in that moment, I saw my mama the way Charlene probably did.

It was like looking at a stranger.

Red spots blotched up her neck from where she'd been rubbing at it. The hand not digging into her pocket was twitching, twitching, twitching, and about to pull a button off her jacket. She wasn't looking me in the eye. Mama didn't even *want* to see the Bird Room. Not even for *me*.

My insides went just as cold and heavy as a slimy lump of yellow clay.

That line from Mr. Bob's letter echoed in my head. *There's some things you just can't change.*

Mr. Bob was right. I couldn't change my mama. She didn't want to change.

Before that thought even had a chance to seep all the way in, Brian hustled up and steered Mama toward the car. "We can talk about this later. Now we all need to hit the road."

Mama's hand reached out. She pulled me toward the car. But my legs stood stock-still.

"Mama, I can't go to Memphis with you." My voice felt like it was coming from someplace outside of me, someplace I didn't know.

"Sure you can, baby. Just get in the car. It'll all be okay. We'll buy you some new clothes at the mall."

"No, Mama, I can't."

"It'll be fun. Brian will take good care of us." Mama brushed her hand against her stomach.

I took a hard, dry swallow and reached into my pocket. "This was under the tanager painting you gave me." I held out the doogaloo.

Mama's eyes lit on the lightbulb carved in that coin, and her cheeks rose up in a quivery smile. "My baby, she always could find the beauty in things. Didn't I tell you, Brian?" She started to give it back.

I closed her hand around it. "You keep it. You can visit me anytime, Mama. Anytime you want to see me and that room."

Mama took three deep breaths. Thick tears welled in her eyes. "You sure you'll be okay?"

"I'll be fine." My ears were buzzing so loud it hurt.

"I'm sorry, Mama." I choked out the words. "I'm sorry for what I said that night before you left. I didn't mean it."

For one sliver of a second, Mama's eyes met mine. "I know you didn't, baby. I'm sorry, too. I wish I could just . . ."

She studied that cricket I'd drawn in the dirt.

I felt like a soda can that's been shook too hard. Everything swirled in different directions inside me—loving my mama and being mad at her for leaving me. I couldn't choose what thought to hang on to. I was hating myself for not being able to change things and a tiny bit proud of myself for coming to know it, and scared of what it was that I was about to do. All that swirling had me dizzy, and I just wanted to get away from myself, but I couldn't do it. I was stuck just as bad as that fish in the trap.

"It'll be okay, hon." Brian said it like he'd already used that line about a thousand times that day. "You can always visit. We'll send her money, like you said." Brian guided

Mama toward the car. "She sure is pretty, same as you. You ought to be proud."

Mama brought the doogaloo to her cheek and held it there. Then she smiled that smile that used to light up the room and me, both at the same time. "Yes, I am."

They piled into a silver sports car that wasn't built for dirt roads. Mama laid her fingers against the glass. She mouthed the word *Bye* and they drove off.

What have I done?

Dust from Brian's car rained down on my skin in tiny flakes, making everything real.

I'd almost died to get to Mama.

And now I'd just let her go.

CHAPTER 45

POSSIBILITIES

I kicked at Brian's tire tracks so hard, I like to fell over.

Then I saw the shadow. It was in the no-doubt-about-it shape of a tanager. It was formed from those two interlocking parts of the headstone. That tanager shadow wavered in the slanty sunlight, looking ready to fly.

Charlene chirped. At least she was still with me. We studied that shadow.

Hope is the thing with feathers. That line from Emily Dickinson popped into my head.

Here was a tanager not afraid to take chances. A tanager not afraid to stand out.

A tanager that flew wherever its hope feathers took it.

Bit by bit, all the things spinning around in my head started to take a blurry shape.

I'd come out to these woods to find the Bird Room for Mama.

Maybe I'd gotten something for myself, too.

I'd made it through thieving raccoons, through the ice storm and the snakebite. I'd fed myself from these woods. I'd protected Charlene. I'd kept the both of us alive.

No matter what people said about Mama, she'd made me into the person who'd done all that. And that was something.

I thought about what Miss V. had said about Mama being more than what those neighbors thought. Miss V. was right. My mama *did* contain multitudes. What those neighbors said about Mama wasn't who my mama was. And it wasn't who I was, either. I was my own, whole person. And *I* could decide what it was I wanted to do.

Everything I'd thought about doing had Mama right at the center.

I'd taken a lot of chances to find my mama. Maybe it was time to start taking chances on *me*.

Charlene chirped on my shoulder, and my mind started to swirl again with maybes, one right after another. Then somehow, all of a sudden, all those maybes started to feel a little bit like possibilities.

When I finally made up my mind, it took the both of us by surprise.

"Pack your things," I told Charlene. "We're heading to the Stokes School."

CHAPTER 46

IT'S A MIRACLE

"Well, that settles it," Miss V. said when I told her all that had happened. "You'll just have to spend a lot of time here with Percy and me." Percy bounced over and slobbered up my face like I was the best thing he'd ever tasted.

Miss V. handed me the key to the Bird Room. I closed my hand tight around it. Me and Charlene, we could visit that room whenever we wanted.

"I've already called the museum," Miss V. said. "They're over the moon about so many paintings. They need to work out the details, but they said they want to buy them all and create a special exhibit. We can go visit it together. And the Bird Room is getting a new roof."

205

So we had a plan.

Aunt Belinda was another story. I needed to settle things between us.

When I showed up on Aunt Belinda's doorstep the next day, the first words out of her mouth were, "You ought to be ashamed of yourself for scaring me that way. Running off without telling me goodbye."

"You left *me*." I was ready to fight.

But soon as I was inside, she pulled me into a hug. She squeezed me hard enough to make me think she might really mean it. "I'm just so glad you're back."

I couldn't say anything. Her Wanda's Classy Lady hair spray was near about choking me to death. For once, though, it smelled sort of good.

She grabbed hold of my arms. "Let me look at you." She wrinkled her nose. "Where have you been? You're thin as a rail, and you look like you've been sleeping with the dogs. Let's get you cleaned up. You had me worried sick."

Then her eyes went wide as she looked out the window behind me.

A white van was raising up a dust cloud on the driveway. It turned the curve, and we both sucked in our breath when we recognized the lettering on the side—DEERFIELD BAPTIST CHURCH. The van crunched to a stop on the gravel. Pastor Dudley, Ms. Mary Beth, and the whole youth group poured out. "We came to offer you some comfort, Sister Belinda," Pastor Dudley said.

Aunt Belinda stepped in front of me, opened the door, and held up my hand. "It's a miracle. Our Cricket has returned!"

Little Quinn, Jackson, and Clay scampered out of the bedroom. Them and the church youth group crowded around me. Aunt Belinda kept backing up until we were all shuffling around in the living room. Pastor Dudley, Ms. Mary Beth, and everybody else but Aunt Belinda eye-balled me the way folks gawked at that five-legged calf at the county fair. I stared right on back. I didn't even try to explain what I was doing with a full-grown cricket on my shoulder.

"Where are my manners? Sit down, sit down, everyone. Make yourselves at home." Aunt Belinda fluttered about, pulling in extra chairs from the dinette set and side-kicking action figures under the couch.

I just stood still and let her try to clean up her own mess.

She pointed to the recliner with a hand wearing Mama's aventurine ring. "Look, Cricket, we saved a seat just for you. We knew you'd be back someday, the good Lord willing."

The sight of that ring riled me back up. Little Quinn grabbed my hand. "Yeah, Cricket. We made your bedroom even better. We've been using it for the coolest rec room you ever—"

Aunt Belinda clamped down on his shoulder. "Give her a chance to catch her breath. After all she's been through."

Pastor Dudley smacked his hands on his knees and leaned forward. "Sister Cricket, you've got to tell us just exactly what you *have* been through. How'd you ever end up away from your family?"

Aunt Belinda got the panic-filled eyes of a fish flapping on a cutting board.

I took a step toward the recliner, but I didn't sit down.

Aunt Belinda laid the back of her hand against my forehead. "The poor thing is exhausted. We should let her rest."

The youth group wasn't buying it. The youngest girl, Renata Terry Jane, raised her hand. "So, where've you been, and how'd you get back?"

That look again from Aunt Belinda.

The biggest part of me wanted to call Aunt Belinda out, to do it right in front of Pastor Dudley, Ms. Mary Beth, and the whole youth group, too. She'd tried to send me off to Great-Aunt Genevieve's. She'd lied to the whole town.

She *deserved* what she had coming—getting locked up in jail for lying to the police, for not telling them how she'd left me in that grocery store.

So what if that left Little Quinn, Jackson, and Clay without a mama. *I* didn't have a mama *or* a daddy around, either one.

The anger rose up so hot, it burned my skin hairs.

"Well, as a matter of fact . . . ," I began. I cut my eyes over at Aunt Belinda. She could see in my face what I was about to do.

I'd just let her squirm a minute before I did it.

But there was her fish-on-a-cutting-board look again. The look of a fish that'd stopped thumping. A fish who'd given up.

In my head, I pictured Mr. Bob walking a thousand miles to get back home to his family. I remembered all those miles I'd walked to try to get Mama back.

I thought about Aunt Belinda putting supper on the table every night, rain or shine.

I thought about her telling me I was family and taking me in.

I sucked in a deep breath—and got a big whiff of Aunt Belinda's fake French vanilla potpourri. And as soon as that smell hit my nose, I knew this one sure thing—I wasn't the same person I was back when I slumped around Aunt Belinda's house.

Being in the woods *had* changed me. It taught me what I was made of. Something that could rise above all the mess Aunt Belinda had made.

Nothing I could do to Aunt Belinda would take what I'd learned away from me. And trying to send Aunt Belinda off to jail wouldn't bring back Mama or Daddy, either one.

I got to thinking quick.

"Welllll . . ." I drew out the sound. "I know I shouldn't have done it, but I went camping by myself, and I got lost and ran out of matches and I was near about to freeze to death. But then I remembered that Wanda's Classy Lady vanilla lip balm that Aunt Belinda gave me. I spread it on some dead leaves and banged two rocks together and got a spark, and I got a fire and I kept that fire going until I could find enough food in the woods and find my way back here."

Every eye was on me. I was on a roll, and I couldn't resist the part that followed. "And here I am today, living proof of the power of Aunt Belinda's beauty products. Aunt Belinda was so happy to see me, she told me she'd give me Mama's lucky aventurine ring. Isn't that right, Aunt Belinda?" I held out my firm and steady palm.

Aunt Belinda didn't say one single word. She just twisted off that ring, gave it a tight-mouthed kiss, and dropped it in my hand.

Pastor Dudley sprang up and laid his hand on my shoulder. "And now Cricket's back with us. All that praying, I knew it would pay off." He held out a Thelma's Cash 'n' Carry grocery bag and untied the handles to show crumpled bills and quarters. The bills were mostly ones, but there were fives, tens, and even some twenties and fifties inside. "We were taking up a collection for a reward for Cricket's safe return. Now that Cricket is back, you might as well have it. After all you've been through." He handed the bag to Aunt Belinda.

"No, we couldn't," Aunt Belinda protested.

But the pastor and Ms. Mary Beth just smiled. The youth group started nodding. "Take it, take it."

"It's unanimous," Pastor Dudley said. "We insist."

Aunt Belinda took the bag gently, the way you'd handle eggs. "Thank you so much. I'm sure we can find a way to put it to good use for our dear Cricket."

Dollywood, here she comes.

But Aunt Belinda looped the handles over my wrist. "For art supplies," she said.

I sucked in a deep breath. Money was tight all over, and the whole church family had raised this money. For *me*. And now everybody wanted me to have it. I started to look up at the ceiling to keep myself from bawling like a baby.

Then I realized it—I knew these folks. And these folks knew me. They didn't judge me or Mama, neither one. So I didn't even try to turn my head as I swiped at my snotty nose.

Aunt Belinda reached out to hug me again, nearly squashing Charlene.

Charlene leaped out of the way.

She landed on Aunt Belinda's shoulder.

Aunt Belinda got to jumping around, jerking her hands, trying to brush off Charlene.

I lunged forward. Charlene could get hurt.

But Charlene just bounced back on me first chance she got. She was tough. By that time, Aunt Belinda was carrying on so much, she'd worked loose a top button.

"Hot stuff!" Little Quinn was hopping from one foot to the other. "Hot stuff, hot stuff!" He pointed right below Aunt Belinda's collarbone.

Aunt Belinda started pulling the shirt edges together and feeling for the buttonhole.

But it was too late.

"Why would Mama write *Hot Stuff* on her neck bone?" Clay asked.

The youth group started snickering.

Pastor Dudley's mouth turned into a tight-lipped line. Everybody quieted down.

Ms. Mary Beth gathered herself up out of her chair and laid a lily-white hand on Aunt Belinda's shoulder. "Sister Belinda will tell us when she's good and ready." There was the slightest hint of a wink at me. "And I, for one, can't wait to hear it."

They packed up and left.

Aunt Belinda sent the boys to play in the woods behind the house.

So it was just me and Charlene and Aunt Belinda. Charlene cowered inside my collar. Aunt Belinda started straightening up the living room.

I handed Aunt Belinda two empty glasses for the dishwasher. "You shouldn't have been so hard on Charlene. She's one of God's creatures, too. All she wanted to do was say hello."

"I don't keep company with bugs." Aunt Belinda swiped at the edge of the coffee table with the hem of her shirt.

She ran her eyes up and down me. "You must be exhausted. Let's go fix up your room. And you've got an awful lot of schoolwork to catch up on."

"Yes, ma'am."

Aunt Belinda turned the knob to the bedroom.

Game pieces covered the bed. Used gym socks and sour yogurt smells wafted through the air.

My duffel bag lay over in the corner. I swung it over my shoulder. Aunt Belinda tried to take hold of the handle. "Here, let me help you."

I held the handle firm.

"I'm good."

Aunt Belinda got a guilty look. Then she was the one who started crying. She confessed about Great-Aunt Genevieve. "It was a mistake from the beginning. I never should have let her talk me into it. You're always welcome here, Cricket."

"I'm sorry for what I put you through," I said. I told her about Miss V. I told her about the spring-break program at the Stokes School. I told her I wanted to go back and forth between her and Miss V.'s houses and that nobody would think bad of her, because Miss V. and Daddy were kin.

It took half the afternoon for Aunt Belinda to get used to the idea. But in the end, she called the folks at the Stokes School and told them I was coming. She even promised to go by Thelma's Cash 'n' Carry and drop off the $36.47 I gave her.

Aunt Belinda wanted to give me a ride all the way to Miss V.'s.

Somehow, that didn't feel right. Aunt Belinda and Miss V. could get to know each other some other time. It just felt fitting for me to go back to Miss V.'s the way I had come—walking through the woods. I let Aunt Belinda drop me off at the dirt road.

Aunt Belinda pulled me into another tight hug. "You do me proud, now."

I couldn't tell whether she was telling me not to go off and embarrass the whole family, or talking about what had gone on between us. But she had a deep smile on her face when she said it, the kind that crinkled up her cheeks.

Charlene crawled to the top of my shoulder. "Tell her bye, Charlene." The words were out of my mouth before I realized how they must have sounded to Aunt Belinda.

Charlene let out a half-hearted call.

Aunt Belinda gave me a hard look. "You know, only male crickets chirp like that. This one's a boy."

Well, that was something.

Turns out, Charlene had been keeping some secrets of her own.

I studied that cricket for a minute. Charlene *yant-yanted* so soft, it sounded like my own breath doing the talking.

Boy or girl, she'd always be Charlene to me.

CHAPTER 47

FRIENDS

Me and Charlene spent one last night at Miss V.'s house before it was time to head out to the Stokes School. Percy galloped up to meet us and ushered us to the porch. Miss V. laid out a feast. There was fried chicken and mashed potatoes with gravy and a whole mess of peas. And corn bread to sop up all the juices. That juice still carried the flavor of the dirt those peas had grown in, the dirt I had dug in, the dirt I was getting ready to shake off my shoes, soon as I left for the Stokes School.

After a pecan pie dessert, Miss V. pulled out the paintings.

Every last thing I'd seen in those woods was there on

that table. I was smoothing out a painting of a rooster when I felt something. Another sheet was stuck to the painting.

Miss V. fetched me a carving knife to pry the pages loose.

What I saw sucked the wind right out of me.

Miss V.'s bright eyes stared back at me from the drawing of a girl who looked to be not two years younger than me. The girl's hair was shiny and brown, parted to one side, and curled at her shoulders. That girl had Miss V.'s eyes, all right, but they were different, too. Those eyes looked like they'd never seen so much as a drop of sadness. That girl was smiling past the edge of the picture as if she was expecting something good right around the corner. She was standing next to a wavy-haired boy. He clutched a sketch pad to his chest and stared at the same spot outside the frame. A zinnia-speckled garden stood behind them. A tanager stretched its wings overhead.

There was a scribbled caption: *FRIENDS.*

Miss V. smoothed her fingers back and forth over that drawing. She stroked the lines of the girl's hair and ran her fingers along her own hair.

Five minutes must have passed before she claimed it. "It's me. Bob and me."

We sat at the table for I don't know how long. Miss V. stared at the painting, and I stared at Miss V. *Both* Miss V.'s. For all that had changed in Miss V., she still tipped her chin up at that same angle.

I looked into the face of the boy in that painting. His eyes were the eyes of an artist, sizing things up, deciding what to put in his picture, what to leave out. He sure picked the right things about Miss V., the things that stood up over all those years.

There was one thing that didn't make sense about that painting, though. It was like it was in a made-up world. Miss V. and the boy were standing side by side, but their shadows tilted toward each other, crossing just where the garden began. No real sunlight would put out shadows that way.

That's when I knew: *Only one color but not one size. Stuck at the bottom, yet easily flies.*

"Look, Miss V." I pointed. "A shadow. The answer to your riddle."

She laughed. For three quick seconds, Miss V.'s face relaxed into the face of the girl in the painting. "That son of a gun."

CHAPTER 48

MULTITUDES

Early the next morning, Miss V. sent me and Charlene off with a breakfast of bacon, eggs, biscuits, and pear-and-ginger jelly she swore would settle my nerves.

Soon as he got a look at my duffel, Percy cocked his head at me and started whining.

Miss V. petted him and handed me the green-duck postcard from the back of the picture frame. "Remember, you belong at that fancy school just as much as anyone."

And I reckoned I did.

I leaned into my hug with Miss V.

Then me and Charlene headed out to the highway to meet Aunt Belinda for the drive to the Stokes School.

My feet found the sidewalk, and I didn't look up until we were standing in the shadow of the tree house.

I ran my fingers over the wood me and Daddy had nailed together, the calico heart Mama had painted. I showed it to Charlene all over again and gathered Charlene's box.

As soon as we got to the Stokes School, I'd get Charlene settled in my dorm room, and I'd sketch the tree house. I'd sketch the woods. I'd sketch Miss V. I'd sketch Mama holding the doogaloo, holding a little part of me with her all the way back to Memphis. She could have it there with her until she was ready to come back.

When me and Charlene got to the edge of the highway, the sun was slanting through the treetops, but the air still had a wet feel about it.

It was time to get going. I looked down. I'd twisted Mama's aventurine ring so much, I'd made a little groove for it on my finger.

Then it struck me. Maybe Mama hadn't abandoned the aventurine ring. Maybe she'd left it for me to find, to bring me luck. I tried to get used to that idea. I let it wallow around in the love and the mad inside me. It started to settle, and I knew. I didn't have to choose between loving Mama and being mad at her for leaving. I was big enough to do both. Maybe *I* contained multitudes, too.

That thought bounced around in me, and something funny happened. I started to feel lighter. It felt like a little bit of weight flaked off me with each and every step. And as for the knuckle-sized knot that was still left, well . . . I was starting to feel like I just might be strong enough to carry it now.

Yant, yant, YANT, yant. Yant, yant, YANT, yant. Charlene's family was going strong in the woods by the highway.

I could feel Charlene twitching, getting ready to join in.

In that instant, I knew just exactly what I had to do.

I just didn't want to do it.

Taking my time, I picked out a spot in a clump of wood violets. Heart-shaped leaves clustered around the purple blooms and dangled tiny, clear dewdrops. I eased Charlene onto the tallest stem and stroked her across the back. "It's okay, Charlene. You go answer them."

Charlene waited the longest time to see if I really meant it.

She tasted the dew on the violet. She edged one foot after the other down the stem.

She let out a quiet *yant.*

Right away, the woods answered her back.

She leaped.

Yellow-veined wings, so fine you could see right through them, opened across her back.

They floated her clear over the honeysuckle vines. Charlene *soared,* just as graceful as one of Mr. Bob's tanagers.

221

I knew it was way too early for it, but I could swear I smelled gardenias.

Charlene's music came so fast and sure, it was like she'd been storing it up the whole time.

Before my feet ever hit the blacktop, I knew that music was going to call me back soon, too.

But first, I had me a little bit of soaring to do of my own.

AUTHOR'S NOTE

The idea for this story began when I was almost Cricket's age. I lived in the real ghost town of Electric Mills, Mississippi, while my family's home was being built on land that used to be part of the horse pasture for the town. I spent a lot of time exploring the woods and encountering signs of the town that had once been there. Electric Mills was the site of one of the first electric lumber mills in the United States. Established in 1913, the town had a hospital, a theater, beautiful homes, an ice cream parlor, offices, schools, and a church. The town produced its own power and was said to be "the brightest town south of St. Louis" during its time. It even had its own currency.

When all the timber had been harvested, most of the town was removed, but a few structures remained.

Growing up, I was intrigued by the thick concrete sidewalks that wove through overgrown woods, and the scattered concrete pillars that had once supported large homes. I made up stories about the people who'd lived there. In writing this book, I changed some details of the town and the natural world that Cricket encounters, and you can read about those differences at my website, JoHackl.com.

The riddle in the story is one that I have heard over the years.

The characters in this book are all invented, including Mama. Mental health issues affect many people, and stigma often keeps them from getting effective treatment, as it did for Mama. Getting effective treatment and support are key, and in the Additional Resources section you can find out where to learn more and where to take the StigmaFree pledge.

Although this novel is a work of fiction, the secret room and the artist in this book were inspired by my favorite artist, Walter Inglis Anderson. I was born near Ocean Springs, Mississippi, where Anderson did much of his work. My father told me stories of how one of his friends sometimes carried Anderson in his later years by boat to and from nearby Horn Island, where the artist camped out, drawing and painting.

Like the fictional artist in this story, Anderson was called Bob by his family. After Anderson's death, a room called the Little Room was discovered in the cottage where he lived in Ocean Springs. The walls of this room were painted to reflect a day on the Mississippi Gulf Coast, and Anderson oriented the paintings to interact with the light outside the windows. Today you can visit the Little Room at the Walter Anderson Museum of Art in Ocean Springs. When I stepped inside the Little Room, it took my breath away. This inspired the hidden-room part of Cricket's story.

During his life, Walter Anderson's work was sometimes misunderstood. The extensive murals he painted in the community center in Ocean Springs were controversial, and some people thought they should be painted over. His drawings for a post office mural had to be significantly changed before they were approved. His proposal to paint a courthouse mural in Jackson, Mississippi, was denied. This event inspired the fictional "Some walls aren't for everyone" clue in the book. As far as I know, Anderson did not leave puzzles, riddles, a buried cache of paintings, or a trail of clues. He did, however, leave behind many paintings of the natural world, often on typing paper. He described the hour before sunset as "the magic hour," when "all things are related." This provided inspiration for the "magic hour" clue.

During a difficult period, Anderson spent some time in mental hospitals. In an escape from one hospital, he is said to have tied bedsheets together to lower himself from an upper-floor room and to have used soap to draw pictures of birds in flight along the exterior wall. And he is said to have once walked a thousand miles to get home.

I've long been inspired by Anderson's brilliant artwork, his remarkable resilience, and his commitment to following his own path in his art. His work has been featured in many books, including some of my favorites, listed in the Additional Resources section. Creating art was a central part of Anderson's life, just as it was for the fictional artist in this book, and my hope is that this story will inspire readers to pursue their own art, whatever it may be. As Cricket would say, sometimes you need to start taking chances on yourself.

ADDITIONAL RESOURCES

The Mississippi Museum of Art: msmuseumart.org
The Walter Anderson Museum of Art:
walterandersonmuseum.org
The Art of Walter Anderson, edited by Patricia Pinson
(University Press of Mississippi, 2003)
Birds, by Walter Anderson and Mary Anderson
Pickard (University Press of Mississippi, 1990)
*Fortune's Favorite Child: The Uneasy Life of Walter
Anderson,* by Christopher Maurer, which
includes "An Alternative Perspective" by Walter
Anderson's son John G. Anderson (University
Press of Mississippi, 2003)
The Secret World of Walter Anderson, by Hester Bass,
illustrated by E. B. Lewis (Candlewick, 2009)

For information about mental illness and resources,
visit apa.org and nami.org. To take the StigmaFree
pledge, visit nami.org.

For information about birds, visit audubon.org and the Cornell Lab of Ornithology at birds.cornell.edu.

For additional information about Leonardo da Vinci and his life, visit leonardodavinci.net.

For additional information about Emily Dickinson, her poems, and her life, visit emilydickinsonmuseum.org/for%20kids.

For information about Walt Whitman, visit state.nj.us/dep/parksandforests/historic/whitman/teaching.html.

For a clue trail you can solve using elements you read about in this book, and for information about the real ghost town and the things Cricket encountered on her journey, visit JoHackl.com.

ACKNOWLEDGMENTS

This book was over ten years in the making, and I have more than ten years' worth of people to thank. My family and friends have provided unwavering support and encouragement, and their willingness to brainstorm and to lend their expertise on topics ranging from art history, clue elements, mannerisms of field crickets, mental health, and outdoor survival skills to poetry have been invaluable.

I am grateful to the amazing Tracey Adams and the brilliant Shana Corey and the entire Adams Literary and Random House Children's Books teams for believing in this project and for their work to make it as strong as possible.

This novel began in a class taught by the enormously talented and generous Ashley Warlick, and her insight has shaped this book. I am blessed to live in a creative arts community and have benefited from workshops, conferences, and gatherings hosted by the Emrys Foundation, the Hub City Writers Project, Read Up Greenville, and the Society of Children's Book Writers and Illustrators. My wonderful and talented friend Mark Johnston simply would not let me put this project down, and his persistence, brainstorming, and encouragement all these years have resulted in this book.

My colleagues at Wyche, P.A., provide inspiration every day with their commitment to excellence.

Special thanks to Rachel Baldwin, Kara Barlow, Bill Barnet, Michelle Bigger, Kelly Byers, Terry Grayson Caprio, Rita Christopher, Carla Davidson, Dr. Benjamin Dunlap, Chris Foster, Clyde Fowler, Debbie Fowler, Mary Gentry, Ted Gentry, Vera Gomez, Cary Hall, Nancy Halverson, Vanessa Hilliard, Anna Kate Hipp, Hayne Hipp, Sue Inman, Hannah Jarrett, Jennie Johnson, Lindsay Jones, Beth Kastler, Alex Kiriakides, Suzanne Kiriakides, Ray Lattimore, Wallace Lightsey, Melinda Long, Joanne Markle, Corajane Melton, Renata Parker, Jessica Pate, Joanne Penick, Rebecca Petruck, Glenis Redmond, Peter Reiling, Lauren Roach, Luanne Runge, Ashley Stafford Sewall, Michael Sewall, June Smith-Jeffries, Monte Stone, Irena Tervo, Carol Wilson, Pam Zollman, the Liberty Fellowship staff, and my Liberty Fellow classmates.

I am grateful to critique partners Carol Baldwin, Helen Correll, Caroline Eschenberg, Landra Jennings, Jan Kovaleski, Sheri Levy, Kelly Pfeiffer, and Marcia Pugh and to

Lorin Oberweger for lending their considerable talents to this project.

To make the outdoor survival scenes realistic, I trained on everything from fire starting, shelter building, and water gathering to foraging for edible and medicinal plants with Alex Garcia and Robin McGee. Any errors are my own, and I have a list on my website (JoHackl.com) of the few creative liberties I took with details of the physical world. Dr. Drew Brannon and Dr. Laura Delustro generously provided information on mental health issues, and Dr. Blake Layton Jr. generously provided information on entomology.

I am grateful to the good people of Kemper County, Mississippi, who generously shared information about the history of Electric Mills, and to the late artist Walter Anderson, whose work inspires many people, including me.

Finally, I am grateful to the bighearted community of educators and librarians who have helped me in this project and whose work makes the world better for us all.

JO WATSON HACKL was born in Biloxi, Mississippi, near Ocean Springs, where her favorite artist, Walter Anderson, lived and once painted a secret room. As a child, Jo loved hearing stories about the mysterious artist. When she was eleven, she moved to a real-life ghost town, Electric Mills, Mississippi. Anderson's secret room and the ghost town were Jo's inspiration for this debut novel. Today, Jo lives with her family in Greenville, South Carolina, where she takes to the woods whenever she can. You can find her online at JoHackl.com.